ASSURED DESTRUCTION

By Michael F. Stewart

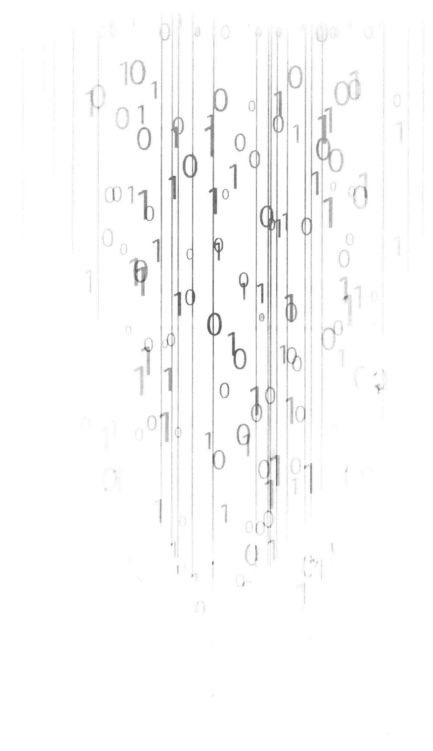

CHAPTER 1

01100100011000010111001001101011011100110110110001010010110
11100110011101100101011100100010111001101110011001010101110100

I F YOU EVER HAVE TO get a job, don't do sales. I hate sales. And this woman is an example of why.

"I am Mrs. Roz Shaftsbury and this hard drive will be destroyed," Mrs. Roz Shaftsbury says.

It's weird how she announces her name, but it does mean something to me. I sit next to her son in half my classes. I've never seen her before, though, and she's dressed in what looks like twenty foxes sewn together and is wearing red heels—I would've remembered—that fox is snarling at me.

I guess because she walked into a dingy warehouse with concrete floors and bare beams and the worst Feng Shui in the world, she assumes we're after her credit card information rather than to earn enough money to buy pizza. But come on, I'm a sixteen-year-old girl, not a ... well ... not a crook.

Roz leans in and stares at me so I know she isn't even asking a question; this is a threat. Erase the hard drive, or else.

I want to salute and say, "Yes, ma'am, your son's secret,

torrent downloading will be deleted forever. His Ivy League future is back on track." But then she'd realize I actually know her son, Jonny Shaftsbury, and I see no point in tipping her off.

"Oh yes, assured destruction," I say. It's what's written on the sign above her head and it helps me keep snide remarks to myself.

"Some computer recyclers just wipe hard drives," Roz adds; her fingernails scrape the laptop casing, sending shrill echoes through the warehouse. "I want this shredded."

With a hint of a European accent, she says it like she researched the subject on Google. If she had, she would also know wiping a hard drive works perfectly well and then it can be reused. But this is a woman wearing foxes, and in retail, the customer is king or ... er ... dark, evil, dead-fox queen.

I point to the shredder, which squats in the corner; it works like a paper shredder but instead of chewing up paper it munches metal. *Chop-chop* is spray painted across its lip.

"Good," she replies, but her hand lingers.

I slide the computer off the counter with a smile and carry it over to the shredder for show. Shaftsbury forks over cash—this woman really doesn't want to leave a trace—it all feels ridiculously covert. I narrow my eyes and hunch my shoulders as if I'm doing something shady.

She huffs and stomps out, twirling her foxes and leaving the smell of her sugary perfume behind. I stand nonplussed. I would have thought she'd want to see the shredder do its work. At least take the certificate of destruction.

I hate sales.

If she wasn't such a bitch, I probably would have popped the hard drive in the shredder, hit the big green button, and assured the destruction of the last few years of Jonny's life. But since I know Jonny doesn't have a chance of making it into an Ivy League school, I don't feel too guilty about checking under the hood to see if it is indeed *the* Jonny Shaftsbury from my high school.

In every kid's hard drive are pieces of themselves, which, if someone is prepared to take the time, can be puzzled back together to live again on what I call the Shadownet. That someone happens to be me.

Hobby? Art form? Sad, pathetic plea to garner friendship, even virtually? Sure, I am guilty on all counts. Maybe I'm even addicted to it. I can pick apart the private lives of others and don't need to worry about what they think about me, or whether the profiles I create for them are going to walk out one day and never come back like my dad did. Shadownet is my permanent family. The only thing I can be sure will stick around.

"Janus, why aren't you working?" The voice of my mother rings with the sing-song tone she uses when she senses I'm about to do something wrong. She's in the back playing with money.

"I am working. Don't harass your unpaid labor," I return in my own sing-song. She has a beautiful voice, though, and mine is like that woman's fingernails on the casing.

"Room and board qualifies as paid, deary," she continues in a fun, easygoing lilt. I love my mom.

Luckily a doctor came in an hour before Jonny's mom, so I pop the shells off his computers, pull the hard drives, and run the shredder. It makes a series of clunks until the hard drives catch in the teeth, then it's like listening to a car crash in slow motion, metal sheering and plastic splintering. I cover my nose at the reek of lubricant and acrid metal. My mom will hear it and never know that one more hard drive didn't quite make it into Chop-chop. For now, I tell myself, choking down the guilt.

Poking about the new laptop, I can see it isn't old—three or four years—but then I'm not hoping for baby pics. I want secrets. Secrets are power. I first realized how powerful when my mom wouldn't tell me why my dad walked out on us. I wonder about it every day. And about what he's doing right now and whether he thinks of me. The hard drives I fail to destroy are my secrets, and no one knows about them, especially not my mom.

I slip the hard drive into the front pocket of my overalls and smile at the next person, who lugs a behemoth of a television he probably paid ten grand for a decade ago. He now has to pay us to take it off his hands.

Finally, it is eight o'clock, and I can quit. My mom's still in the back office with her head in a spreadsheet. I know we're not making much money, but Assured Destruction is all that keeps us from the food bank. Still, we manage. I work a lot of hours and have ever since my dad abandoned us.

I pat the hard drive in my pocket and dream about what secrets I will find within its folders. It being the end of the month, I've got a couple more hours before my mom rolls away from her computer and comes looking for me. She's in a wheelchair due to her Multiple Sclerosis, otherwise known as MS.

I lock the doors to the warehouse store and wheel the television and shells of computers to the staging area at the back. Fenwick, our forklift driver and all around handy dude, will skid them and add them to the next shipment out. Fenwick looks like a pro wrestler ten years after retirement—built like a truck but starting to fall apart. I haul some of the lighter items off the cart to make his life easier but balk at the television.

The whole place is filled with racks of old computers, televisions, and electronics. But we don't actually recycle, not anymore; we do better just collecting a fee for the drop off and letting the larger companies do the hard work. The only business where we still actually do anything is destruction. People don't like to think you're shipping their data anywhere and all it takes is a shredder. I know when a doctor, lawyer, or accountant walks through the door, they're carrying the next pizza I can order.

As I take the stairs to the basement, cool air slides up my thighs. It's like descending to a lake bottom on a hot summer's day. Goosebumps bubble over my arms and I slip on the sweater I leave across my chair. To me the hum of the computers and server is a Buddhist's meditation. Knots at my neck unravel. I sigh and sit in my rolly chair, feeling a little closer to the Internet, which to me is the same as enlightenment. My chair needs to be rolly because I have seven terminals in a ring network. I am like a starship captain: I kick out, the chair rattling over the floor to the first terminal.

From the screen, a cartoon version of me stares back. Black straight hair, overlarge dark brown eyes, pale complexion, and a pointy chin. It looks like me, but without the zits, and in real life my neck isn't only an inch wide.

As I shift the mouse, it takes me to my home blog: JanusFlyTrap. When I built the site, I was trying to think of a cool name and spotted all the wires tangled at the hub of my network like a web. Six other computers all link to mine and to each other. One dysfunctional family. And like any family, each part has its own personality.

On my right is Gumps. Gumps is my conscience, my grandfather, my confidante, my Magic 8-ball, all on the oldest motherboard I've ever seen. The computer is pre–Internet and so Gumps isn't connected to the others, but I still see him as the closest thing I've got to flesh and blood, the only person I can really trust. His display is green, and rather than sporting an avatar, he's just a blinking dash. Don't let appearances fool you, though. He's with it.

I type: *Gumps, 8-ball question: should I search around in Jonny's files?*

I programmed it to recognize key terms I enter. The response is immediate.

Answer: *Janus, the ball is in your court.*

He speaks in idioms, which is nice because it leaves me to interpret his answers however I want. Exactly what I imagine grandparents are for.

I set the hard drive into a casing I have for this purpose and turn on the unit. This could be interesting. A year ago Jonny asked me out and I turned him down, mostly because life was crazy with my mom's illness and with taking care of the business while scraping by at school. Then, just a few months ago, Fenwick caught Jonny snooping around Assured Destruction— it was a bit too close to stalking for me. Jonny could barely look at me in class afterward. If he ever came around again, I joked that Fenwick should feed him to Chop-chop.

On the computer screen, a series of folders appear in the file tree.

I was right. It's Jonny.

Let the fun begin.

CHAPTER 2

01100100011000010111001001101011011100110110110001101001011011
1110011001110110010101110010001011100110111001100101011110100

CAN TELL BY THE HOMEWORK assignments that it's Jonny's hard drive. All his files are still there; Jonny's mom hasn't attempted to erase anything, which saves me a ton of time. With the woman's *or else* still echoing in my head, I scroll around only to hover above a folder marked *Chippy*—Chippy is our computer science teacher. He and I have a mutual hatred of one another. This is not a friendly, competitive dislike; this is an *I can write circles of code around him and he knows it* animosity. In turn, he fails me. All the time.

Sure, he justifies it because I never do the work. His lessons are stupid. He teaches an antiquated programming language that no one ever uses. If he gives us a lesson to program some simple math functionality, I'll give him back a calculator iPhone app instead. But I don't do it in BASIC, so he fails me. It's like being forced to write Latin in English class. I refuse to cave in.

I take my revenge on him online. He suspects who's running *denial of service* attacks on his Dungeons and Dragons blog.

He even accused me once of changing his profile picture to a donkey and spamming him with penile-enlargement offers, but that wasn't me; that was Heckleena.

Heckleena sits two terminals down from JanusFlyTrap. She's a tough cookie—thirty three years old, single, baby clock ticking, no relationship prospects. Rumors about her Special Forces background swirl in the digital ether. Just like people are into whips and chains in the bedroom, some people like to be heckled in public. Lots of them. Her Twitter followers love how she bites the heads off of everyone else. I created Heckleena to keep myself sane during a tough period in my life—my first profile on Shadownet. I use her Twitter feed to let out all my anger and frustration.

I go to my Twitter page. I scan everything and DM Heckleena: *@Heckleena I've got Jonny on the hard drive, wanna see?*

I scoot to her terminal; her avatar's a set of screaming lips.

@JFlyTrap Why would I care about your piddly life and stupid friends? #pleaseunfollowme

I don't even know what she's going to say until I type it! It's what her bio says too: *I don't like you, please don't follow me.* An example of how well reverse psychology can work.

Having all these virtual Twitter accounts might seem weird, but it's freeing. I can be who I want. On the Internet, I'm not some drudge of a retail clerk. I'm not the only thing keeping my mom and me from starving. Besides, real people and real relationships end badly. Eventually, always.

I know what some psychologist would say, that these terminals are all me, and they are, or parts of me. But they're also more real than a doctor might think. I'm Dr. Frankenstein and online Shadownet has a pulse.

In a flurry of new activity Heckleena types:

@Sue369 Saw pic of new baby—can you put it back?

@Wendyshawmister The Internet is not solely for LOLcats—

post one more and your felines are roadkill.

Heckleena finishes with a post to all her followers: *Oh Lord, it is hard to be humble when you are perfect in every way.*

Back at my terminal I search Jonny's pics. There's one where he looks off his rocker—heavily lidded eyes, drooling mouth, a total zombie. I paint a big black rectangle over his eyes and fire it over to Heckleena, who sends back an *LOL* and retweets the pic to her followers with: *Ottawa's education system at work!*

Ha! Maybe Jonny's here to stay. The first thing I need to do when creating a profile for Shadownet is to create an avatar, a visual representation of his online presence. Maybe a jester? Every family needs some comic relief. But I've got other stuff to do before I recreate Jonny and I'm not a hundred percent sure he's a great fit—it's like asking myself if I want a little brother.

In my inbox I've got messages from flesh and blood people, lots of them, most are just fans thanking me for the free iPhone apps I make. A couple are from wannabe boyfriends. I seem to attract guys who—just because we can talk tech—think I'm into them. Other boys just find me weird. Why can't I get a real guy? The only boys I like are in senior year. I'm taller than most boys in my class and the ones I'm not taller than would be like dating coat racks, well ... most of them.

My mom says I'm threatening. But only once did I tell a guy to stay away or face having his Internet surfing habits spread across the school. It's not like I would have done it.

Oh my—here's an email from a would-be suitor that has a poem:

> Your hair like firewire.
> Mind like a terabyte drive and your dual core processors ...
> My heart is a cursor beating for your fingertips.

OMG. If the kid hadn't sent it anonymously I would make sure everyone saw this. Hair like firewire? Mine's straight and glossy black and I thought one of my better features, until now. Credit given for the last line. I sigh. I don't have time to sort through all my email and I'm growing drowsy, my eyelids drifting lower as the combination of too much homework and too many hours at the cash catches up to me. One message shocks me back; it's from my mom: *Dear Janus, Have you remembered our little deal?*

Our deal: Pass your courses or bye-bye computer time. Hmm.

I have a math test tomorrow, but I'm good at math. English essay due as well. That I'm not so good at and I haven't started the book ... who wants to read some book whose author offed herself after writing it? But if I fail this essay, I fail the semester.

Crap.

I used a free essay site for the last one and shouldn't push my luck. I don't have much choice, though ... not when I have to work a four-hour shift most nights—and so I set about cobbling a combination of Wikipedia entry, cum-free essay, and Amazon reviews together. It's mindless work, although it shouldn't be, and I keep drifting back to Jonny's files. And then I'm searching through them ...

Secrets aren't the only reason to dig around in hard drives. I also learn a lot about myself. I'm not as strange as I thought. Everyone thinks they look sort of kooky ... other than Ellie Wise, who even I have to admit is pretty. Everybody has a guy or girl she or he hasn't talked to, but wants to. Rebuilding a person's profile isn't just fun, it's cathartic.

What ho! Do my eyes deceive me? I'm staring at a folder tree with a whole series of dates, one folder for each day. Is this a treasure above all others, held deep in the bowels of Jonny's hard drive?

A journal! It is!

Jonny has a diary!

Only one of my terminals has a diary and that's Frannie. Frannie is ten, and her journal is this naïve stroll across the lawns of rich, white, urban Canada. I use her naiveté for pranks. Like, she has a fetish for replying to spam—the emails that ask for help to win a lottery prize, or to collect an inheritance? Just for fun she once tried to help a bunch of widowed Nigerians by copying them all on the same email so they could share their common need for foreign assistance in recovering tens of millions of dollars.

Frannie comes across so startlingly innocent that the Russians actually believe her—one actually asked to speak with her via SKYPE, reminding me that there are real people at the other end of these fiber optic cables.

I agreed, of course, but when I answered the SKYPE call I didn't turn on my webcam. He wore silver wraparound shades and this heavy gold necklace. Muscles bulged all over him, and hair tufted out his collar. Obviously Russian.

If that wasn't enough, he spoke with a heavy accent and, when he removed his glasses to peer at the screen, his eyes were completely black, as if they were just the pupil. Still gives me the shivers. I didn't say a thing, just waited until he swore at the computer and disconnected. I know what you're thinking, but I route my server off a half dozen other servers, so there's no way they can trace me.

Given Jonny is sixteen, I'm willing to bet his journal is a little more risqué than Frannie's. I open the first entry and gasp.

Looks like Jonny can draw.

There I am on page one … he actually took the trouble to scan this stuff in.

And page two. I'm drawn in pastels here with an overlong neck and blank staring eyes.

The sound of my mom's wheelchair as it rolls across the warehouse floor warns me that she's coming. She can never sneak up on me. One day I'll fix the squeaking, but for now it's handy. Besides, there are bigger things that need repairing around here.

Page three: doodles of an alien.

Page four: me again. A penciled profile of my face, blemish free, nose snubbed upward and eyes shut as if I'm enjoying something. It's hyper realistic. Shivers rattle down my spine. One thing is for certain, Jonny's interest in me hasn't waned.

I don't know how to do it without tipping him off that I have his old computer, but when I get to school, Jonny and I are going to have words.

The drawings confirm it; Jonny deserves a spot on Shadownet. It's time for me to work my magic. It's time for Jonny to take his rightful place. He should be honored.

"Janus, come up for dinner," my mom calls from the top of the stairs.

"Half an hour?" I ask. Half an hour is barely enough time to get started but it's the most I can demand. The squeaks slowly roll away, and then the gears of the elevator crank over as it descends to pick my mom up.

Thirty minutes for a Jonny makeover. Let's go.

CHAPTER 3

01100100011000010111001001101011011100110110110001101001010110
11100110011101100101011100100010111001101110011001010101110100

Each member of Shadownet needs its own hardware. I could house them all on a single computer, I suppose, but there's something comforting in the physical presence of so many machines. We're a community and every member has their own quirks. Frannie's keyboard is a bit sticky. The mouse for JanusFlyTrap doesn't record every click. And a black bar runs vertically down Heckleena's screen where the pixels don't light. I even dressed them up for Halloween.

To complete the physical setup, I take an old computer tower from a rack of them we save for resale and slot Jonny's hard drive inside, screwing in the housing to secure it using tiny screwdrivers. I power up the dual-core processors and attach a monitor, one of the old tube kind—people aren't recycling many flat screen monitors just yet. So far it looks like almost every other computer you've seen.

I draw a deep breath, taking in the subtle scents of heating fiberglass, silicon, and rare metals. I don't connect to the

Internet or to Shadownet yet, I'm always worried about viruses and the like. I probably shouldn't even have used JanusFlyTrap to peek through the hard drive.

At this point it's like I'm trying on clothes at the store. I may like the look of them on the rack, but I haven't bought anything. To really get invested I need a visual. Jonny requires some way to represent him on the screen that isn't a real picture of him. This will be Jonny's avatar, like Heckleena's screaming lips or Frannie's doll head. You get the idea.

I slip the same picture I sent to Heckleena into an application that takes images and turns them into cartoons. I tap the desk, waiting for the result. With a little *Ta-Da!* sound, the caricature pops on to the screen and I gasp. The cartoon that looks back at me is ... well ... hot. Not even cute: hot.

The program melded Jonny's shaggy hair and gave a twinkle to his deep brown eyes. Maybe the spark was always there and I just didn't see it? With a face clear of blemishes, he doesn't look so foolish; full lips curve in a smile more wicked than silly.

I set the image as his background and screensaver. I catch myself staring and shake my head. It'll represent him on his social media accounts too. Before I create those, though, he must have a screen name ... um ... Imsohot? Mr. Jonny Rose? Touch-him-and-die? I need to research this.

At the heart of any profile is the username and avatar I choose. Sometimes I go with my gut, what I need it to be, but other times like this one I try to understand the person within the bits and bytes. I delve back into his files. My first stop are his photos and videos. He's got a billion pictures, mostly of graffiti, and I imagine him being some sort of gangster. Maybe the school is his turf and he deals drugs to support his family? Speaking of which, he has a little sister. She's all of three feet tall, freckled, and her mop of hair is even longer than his. She looks happy in a grubby, *I get to roll in mud* sort of way.

The latest shots are from the summer, nothing more recent. What happened a few of months ago? There are no pics of Foxy Lady either. She's probably the type who's never home or ignores the kids. But this is about Jonny and his new home—trapped on Shadownet. Jonny the ... gangster? No, that's not quite right.

I click on a video and clap my palm over my mouth. Jonny sits at a picnic table and strums a guitar. He's not great and the guitar is out of tune, but his voice is clear and strong. So he's into music—and a lot of the same groups I enjoy. I scan his Internet cache and see he's on some music forums, likes horror movies. His browsing history ended three months ago, too. It must have been when he received his new computer.

So, music, horror, graffiti. Somehow Jonny the Jester doesn't fit the cute guy staring out at me. I avert my eyes from his gaze, know it's ridiculous, and so force myself to stare back. Jonny, Jonny ... hmmm. I start humming the tune he was singing using his name as the only lyric.

The last date in his journal is August 23rd:

Why can't my parents understand my art? It's the totally most important thing to me. It's how I think and get crap out of my head. If I didn't paint, I'd explode!

Jonny paints? Jonny Picasso, the *artiste*—no, there's more of edge to him. I'm waiting for my *aha* moment. Frannie's came when I went to bed and saw an old doll from my long lost childhood. So I named her after my doll and took a photo of it for her avatar. Maybe she represents me trying to get back that time—the time when I had a family and a healthy mom?

A few years ago, when my mom was first diagnosed, she was really sick and couldn't even get out of bed. Then my dad left us. I guess he forgot the part of the marriage vows that promised to support her *in sickness and in health*. I had to take care of the world after that. I ordered pizza every night for weeks and covered for my mom by running the business. We almost lost it. You try doing your parent's taxes.

One day, soon after my dad left, my mom asked me to shred a hard drive. Her hand was shaking and it was all really weird. So I plugged it into a casing, of course, and learned it was from my dad's computer. Looking at the pictures on it I've never cried so much in my life. I couldn't just delete it, so I rebuilt a computer around the hard drive and connected it to mine. Other than the pics, I've never looked at the files and emails. One day I might, but for now it's a vow I've kept. My mother will be the one to tell me why he left.

There's a picture of her on the desktop and it's staring at me now: She's standing on one leg, arms outstretched like an airplane, balancing and grinning from ear to ear. One day, maybe sooner than later, she'll be gone. At least I'll have this.

I read on in Jonny's journal and try to ignore my own pain, but reading about his frustration causes mine to bubble up.

Maybe I should paint the house, maybe that would show them! I can just imagine them walking out the door in the morning to find my art covering every inch of the walls—even the roof! The house would be a paradise.

Paradise.

I search for the word in his journals and find fifty-seven references. The username *Paradise* is taken on Twitter so I search his files for a favorite number and discover that his is 57, which is too weird. Paradise57 it is.

Staring into the cartoon eyes of Paradise57's Facebook profile (which I immediately friend), suddenly his doodles of me don't seem quite so creepy. I feel closer to Jonny with our shared annoyance with our parents. I set up a Twitter account for him and a blog, The Art of Paradise, and introduce Jonny to the various feeds. *Hey everyone check out @paradise57says— he's a nube.*

I lean back in the chair, wondering what good can come of this, wondering who I'm exploring here, a new side of me, or am I profiling a boy like a crime profiler recreates a murderer? On Twitter Paradise57 follows a hundred Tweeple who I know always follow back.

It's alive!

Who am I? He tweets.

"Janus?" my mom calls through the intercom. I sigh. "Come upstairs."

"In a minute, I have to feed the cats," I scream loud enough for her to hear, then listen to the silence.

I pick up the cable that will tether Paradise57 to Shadownet and hesitate. Frannie, Heckleena, Hairy, Tule, JanusFlyTrap, Gumps, my mom and dad these are my family. They've been with me anywhere from months to years. They have photo albums, blog followers, YouTube channels—they represent hundreds of hours of dedicated work. They're me and they're not going anywhere. People can leave. People can die. Paradise57 isn't me yet. He's Jonny. I turn to Gumps, who's impartial since he isn't connected to the others.

Gumps, 8-ball question: does Paradise57 belong?

Answer: *Beauty is in the eye of the beholder.*

I take a look at Paradise57's manga-big eyes and lose myself in them for a minute.

I plug him in.

"Welcome, Paradise57," I say. "Be careful. Annoy me and I will unplug you."

He sends a tweet to Heckleena: *Why not make the world a beautiful place? A Paradise ...*

I smirk as I rattle over to Heckleena's terminal. *Why don't I chop you into 57 pieces and you tell me what paradise looks like ... @Paradise57says*

Yes! I need Jonny.

I shove my chair back, climb the stairs to the warehouse, and shoulder open the rear door for the nightly cat feeding. Six cats are already here, keeping to the shadows, but I can see them padding over the gravel. Every night I put out a bowl of food. I tell my mom it's so they don't yowl all night long, but really, it's nice to run my hands through the fur of a cat sometimes, even if that fur is flea and tick ridden.

With the cats happily munching on some Fancy Feast, I climb the stairs to our apartment above the warehouse.

The upstairs was originally offices, and we converted them to a full apartment. If I ever invite friends over for a party, they all have their own offices in which to sleep. As I shove through the emergency exit door, my mom cries out and snaps her laptop closed. I stop cold.

"You frightened me," she says, clutching her laptop to her chest. Her wheelchair is beside her and her legs stretch out on the couch. She's so small she barely dimples the cushions.

I remain in the doorway. "Um ... sorry, I'll thump up the stairs louder next time." She must have expected me to take the elevator, which is noisy and slow.

"Good." She seems mollified and relaxes, wrinkles smoothing from her brow. Her long fingers hook mousy brown hair away from her face.

"What were you doing?" I walk into a large area which would have once been clogged with cubicles and cabinets. Now it is plush-carpeted and filled with two big couches, an armchair, a coffee table, and a dining section replete with IKEA table and chairs. If not for the buzzing fluorescent lighting, it would feel like a real living room.

"Surfing the Web—you know," she says. "Online shopping."

"As if," I say, knowing my mom is not one to shop, online or otherwise. "I can find out the sites you were on in thirty seconds—I don't even need your laptop."

She bristles, eyes widening. "Don't you dare. I deserve my privacy."

I can tell by the straightness of her back: She's hiding something. I decide not to press. And I won't look at her browsing history, either, but I have a hard time not threatening her. It's not that I'm ungrateful; I know my mom can't do as much with the MS, but I never get a thank you from her. I work a minimum of three or four hours every day before homework, more on weekends. I don't get paid for it. I could be designing apps or doing better in school or just being a teenager, maybe even have a boyfriend.

My mom is still clutching the laptop with a white-knuckled grip, as if I can read the hard drive from the doorway.

"I won't go through your stuff," I say.

She swallows and flushes.

"What—?" I ask.

"I was on a dating site." She says it in a rush like if she doesn't she won't be able to get it out.

I clap my palm over my mouth.

"No!" Then I laugh. "My mom is having cybersex!"

Her flush deepens. "I didn't say that."

"I'm kidding, but be careful, please!"

"It is safe," she says. "Actually, I'm really impressed by the people on it."

"Really," I say. "Because they obviously look like the pictures they've sent you and are who they say they are."

She lets the laptop fall to her slender thighs. "Why wouldn't they?"

"Just saying, Mom, you don't know." She's reminding me a little bit of Frannie.

"Funny thing is," she says in a weirdly pensive manner, "I wonder if I like it because of that too. No one can see me. My MS."

"And you're the one who's always telling me to be myself," I say.

She sighs and looks at me with a thin mouth. "Sit down, honey."

I bite my lip and take a spot in the armchair, curling my legs beneath me.

"Up until a month ago I hadn't gone on a date since Dad."

I blink my surprise. She's been on dates in the last month I didn't know about?

"They've come over here," she explains, sensing my distress. "I haven't hidden them from you, but you're always buried in your computers."

They?

"To be honest, I haven't felt very womanly since I was diagnosed, and since your dad ..."

"What? What did Dad do?" I ask. On the day they announced their separation, they had this huge fight over something. I have no idea over what and my mom has never trusted me enough to explain. Afterward, she collapsed into a major depression for a month, and I became the head of the family.

"This isn't about what happened," she says. "It's about how good I feel now that I'm dating again." She blushes even deeper and I'm stunned.

"You could have told me."

She shakes her head a little. "Maybe it's time you went on a few more dates yourself?"

Maybe I am more hurt than I let on, or maybe I'm jealous, but whatever the reason, anger burns through me. "Maybe if I wasn't chained to the store, I could date."

She holds my stare as my eyes water. For once, I wish we could have a conversation without laying on guilt. Her chin drops and she takes a deep breath.

"Okay, honey, I'll try to work some more."

I'm ashamed that I smashed her good mood into a billion fragments and don't trust my voice not to crack. Instead, I nod and head to my bedroom. The label on my door reads *Vice President Sales*. I hate sales and I'm finding it really hard not to hate myself.

A storm is rolling in, and the whole building shakes with each round of thunder.

CHAPTER 4

01100100011000010111001001101011011100110110110001101001011 0
11100110011101100101011100100010111001101110011001010111010 0

G OOD MORNING BEAUTIFUL WORLD, FRANNIE tweets.
Soon the world will end and you all will be let off the hook for your miserable lives #endoftheworld, Heckleena tweets.

Hairy adds his intellectual bit to the conversation: *Prophets do not have a good track record when predicting the #endoftheworld.* I'm standing at the bottom of the steps to my school, fingers dancing over the gorilla-glass surface of my iPhone as I hail the Twitterverse.

What should Paradise57 write? It shouldn't be so hard to come up with ideas.

Good morning, he tweets, and I roll my eyes.

My school is sort of pretty. Red brick, built a hundred years ago for a couple hundred students. A thousand now attend, and the additions are matched to the heritage with a modern touch in the form of a big glass atrium. Unfortunately the expansion ate up most of the sports fields, but I'm not into athletics anyways. Last night's storm has filled the air with a fresh-scrubbed scent and crisp energy.

As I stroll up the twenty steps to the entry, my heart climbs into my throat. Jonny's reflected in the windows; he's right behind me.

"Hey," he says as he walks right past.

He's in through the doors before I can respond.

My lip hurts. I didn't realize I was biting it. Jonny and Jan. JJ. Ugh.

Jonny is cute, and now that I think about it, always doodling and sketching away at the back of the class. His shaggy hair hangs down in front of his eyes.

I'm suddenly very conscious that I chose to wear a skirt this morning. I hardly ever wear skirts or dresses, but here I am on the school steps, cold autumn air blowing over my thighs and through my thin sweater. I steel myself to follow and confront him about his hobby, but suddenly everything dissolves into a shrill whine.

"... break-in? It isn't a *break-in*. This is totally more than a break-in." Ellie Wise's eyes are saucers; she's waggling her phone at her chubby sidekick, Hannah, and looking—for the first time in my living memory—like she hasn't stepped out of a salon. No makeup, frizzy hair—are those clothes even clean? I am desperate to take a picture and seriously wonder if we've entered an alternate world or exchanged brains today.

Ellie's supposed to be on vacation. She's not due back until tomorrow—not that I'm keeping track or anything.

"*Everything* is gone?" Hannah exclaims.

"Everything," Ellie replies.

"That sucks," I say, cutting into the conversation.

Ellie glances up at me, eyes bored. "You wouldn't understand," she says. "They took all our computers and televisions, furniture, clothes. Everything. They took the books off our shelves."

"Audacious," I reply. "That would have taken hours."

"Yeah, our stupid neighbors actually spoke with the thieves, who told them they were movers."

"Terrible," Hannah says.

"Sick," I add, a little impressed.

"Maybe you *would* understand," Ellie says to me with her finger on her chin. "You know what it's like to have nothing. It does suck."

I bristle, but only part of me hates Ellie for these remarks. I tolerate her because she is "Tule"—read Tool—on Shadownet and I let everyone trash-talk her. She's also handy for social reasons. I know she thinks we compete, but we were best friends in elementary school and so hang out with some of the same people. We have a history that ensures I can be with the "in" group, and I admit it I want this sometimes. Especially when a certain boy is around.

"Is that why you're wearing those clothes?" Hannah asks Ellie. "Because all your nice ones are gone?"

And when Hannah says this, I laugh. Ellie's jaw makes a cracking sound as it drops.

"They're not bad—just rumpled," Hannah continues as Ellie lets out an indignant huff and shoves past me. Hannah stays on the steps, looking pained. Ellie doesn't handle insults well, and drawing attention to her ragged appearance isn't smart.

I knew Ellie was on vacation; I had her father's receipts for the flights. He dropped off her hard drive four months ago and from it rose: The Tule. It reminds me that Ellie now has a perfect excuse not to hand in her essay on time. Pretty and lucky. I hate her a little more. I can't imagine what it would be like to be robbed and to lose Shadownet, though—like losing limbs.

#Endoftheworld is here—I've lost all my clothes, they even took my makeup, Tule tweets, and it makes me feel better.

Before heading to class, I call home to check in on my mom;

she has good days and bad days. Today is a good day and that lifts my spirits too. The school is abuzz, but the bell rings and I don't have a chance to talk to anyone to find what about.

Math test is a snap, and by the time lunch arrives, I'm eating a peanut butter and jelly sandwich.

Karl steps into the cafeteria, and I finish my bite, carefully scraping all the peanut butter off my teeth with my tongue. Karl may have a crappy name, but his muscles bulge in places that no other sixteen-year-old's do. I've always been jealous of his relationship with Ellie; they're not boyfriend-girlfriend, they're closer than that. Like brother-sister, always looking out for one another. He's staring at me with sea-colored eyes. My thoughts aren't very sisterly. If he has a peanut allergy, I'm prepared to kill him in order for our lips to touch.

"Hey, Ellie." He waves, and I realize he's not looking at me, but through me. "Heard about the robbery." His hair is so blonde it's almost white. "Need another set of hands to clean up?"

I clear my mouth of the last of the peanut butter. "I'll help too, Ellie, if you need someone." I can't believe I just offered to clean Ellie's house, using time I don't have, helping someone I'm not sure I like.

"Thanks anyways, Jan," Ellie says, "but I can't pay anything."

Back up, sister. This chick is always talking about how poor I am. I smile broadly. "I'll wave my usual fee, just for you."

"Then—?" Her smile widens as she looks to Karl. "Oh." And with a smug look, she gives him a great, long hug and peck on the cheek of thanks. "Looks like I have all the help I need."

Tool. Tool. Tool! I can think of worse words and I'm about to voice my opinion when someone screams: *PIGS!*

I duck before realizing that I'm not actually doing anything illegal.

Two police officers enter the cafeteria and stand before Harry Giannopoulos, a short junior with enough curly brown hair to make his head look like a mushroom cap. Harry also happens to be my *Hairy* on Shadownet. I can't hear what the police say, but if Harry has the right to remain silent, he sure doesn't use it.

"I didn't post naked pictures," Harry says, afro bobbing at the policeman's shoulder. "I didn't! I didn't do it. She's my girlfriend!"

It's quite the show. Easily a hundred kids are gawking, standing on tables, many taking pics with their smartphones. I take one myself. I'll let Heckleena have her say later. #Thingsthatwillnotlookgoodonthecollegeapplication.

Behind, I hear sobbing. Astrid, Harry's girlfriend, slinks into the glass atrium held at the elbow by a female officer.

After Harry's *I didn't do it* does nothing, Harry shuts down, and we all follow him and Astrid into the atrium and down the steps of the school until they enter cruisers slack-jawed and wide-eyed. The way the boys are looking at Astrid curdles the contents of my stomach; I suddenly realize that half of them are trying to picture her naked.

"Show is over," calls Principal Wolzowksi from the top step. But we all know it's so not. "Off to class."

If you've ever had a lockdown or something big happen at your school, you'll know what happened next. Girls are crying … why, I'll never know … guys are chattering and freaking out that they linked to the picture and wonder if they're criminals. Suddenly I realize that tucked into my knapsack is my cut-and-paste masterpiece for English class. I sort of feel as if Harry is a good friend of mine since he's part of the Shadownet. But the reality is I need to get out of class this afternoon and this looks like my chance. In the chaos of Wolzowski trying to herd everyone inside, I slip away.

Strangely, by the time the tires of my wreck of a car crunch over the parking lot of Assured Destruction, I do begin to worry. Two people who are on my network just had terrible things happen to them. Ellie had everything stolen, and Harry's been grabbed by the police for posting child pornography. A coincidence? I shudder and the hair at the back of neck lifts like miniature antennae. The afternoon sun suddenly feels a little pale.

CHAPTER 5

0110010001100001011100100110101101110011011011000110100101110
1110011001110110010101110010001011100110111001100101011110100

"FIRST ELLIE, NOW HARRY AND Astrid," I wonder aloud as I enter Assured Destruction, startling Fenwick. The notes of the Chris Isaak tune he's been singing—*Baby did a bad, bad thing*—die off and he flushes.

I'm home early, and he is still at the cash.

Fenwick is one of those overeducated imports who can't find a better job. I think he has a PhD in something from his former life in Estonia and speaks a dozen languages, but here he handles the register and lifts heavy objects. He's good at that, with his neck like a tree trunk and these meaty hands which could snap *my* neck in a second. I feel guilty because I actually don't know much about him even though he's worked here for almost a year and he's my mom's only other employee. He shakes my hand—always shakes my hand—and it's like gripping a bundle of sausages.

"You're welcome, Fenwick!" I say after he thanks me for letting him off early. "You going home to a wife and kids now or out to find a bride?"

He pauses, face screwed up, and I realize I've insulted him. Maybe his wife and kids are stuck in Estonia? Maybe they're dead. Maybe he killed them! Then his face splits into a grin as the translation registers.

"Not wife and kids. Other job." He shrugs. "Maybe other time?"

Does he think I asked him out? I try to recall what I said and suspect something was lost. "All right then, have fun, hope your back is okay from that TV I left," I say.

He shrugs again and sticks out his lips. He does this often, and I think it means *don't worry about it*. In Italian it stands for whatsamatterforyou?

"I team kettlebell. National Champion 1996."

I blink, itching for Wikipedia in order to look up kettlebell. Instead I nod vigorously until I'm distracted by the bell as a customer enters. Pizza, I think, seeing the suit and tie and a stack of IBM ThinkPad laptops.

As Fenwick leaves, I flash my best smile at the customer.

"Assured destruction?" I ask.

But he shakes his head. "Just recycled, please."

"No confidential documents? Passwords? Medical information? Financial reports?" I add. "Nothing that you'd file under *need to keep confidential* or you'll get sued?"

He pales and I smile inwardly.

"How much?"

"Fifteen dollars a hard drive."

"To turn on your shredder?"

"We'll give you a certificate. You'll have done your due diligence." This last bit always impresses the lawyers and financial types.

It earns me a raised eyebrow and a shake of a head. "Seems like something I can do with my sledgehammer."

I suspect he doesn't have one with him, so I just let silence extend between us.

Finally, he shrugs defeat and sets the laptops down on the counter. "Destruction, then."

I smile and take the five pizzas. Then I write out the certificates so that he has them for his records and hand copies over.

The afternoon has started well so far, but a chill lingers in the cool warehouse. I wrap my arms around me. Five more hours until close.

"I'm going to order a pizza, okay, Mom?" I call, letting her know I'm home.

"No pineapple!" she calls back. She's no fun.

I order the pizza, putting fruit on half, and set to work cracking open the laptops to pull the hard drives. Chop-chop is making spaghetti of them when the door chimes again. I figure it's the pizza, but when I look up, a cop stares me down. I've had enough cops for one day. I shut Chop-chop off and return to the cash.

"I'm looking for Mrs. Rose?" the cop says. A pin on her uniform tells me she's Constable Williams.

She looks Hispanic but speaks without an accent. I search for suspicious challenge in her brown eyes but find none. The officer straightens her shirt, which has ridden up on her bulky gear. What happens if you have big boobs and need to wear a Kevlar vest?

"That's *Ms.* Rose," I reply. "One second." I turn. "Mom! Cop here to see you!"

My mom's chair squeaks with each rotation of its wheels as she emerges from the back room. Between the mousy hair and the chair sounds, I sometimes see her as a little rodent. In a good, cute way. Evidently I take after my father.

"Yes, officer?" my mom asks, rolling up to the counter.

"Have you had Family Planning Clinic as a customer?" the cop demands.

"What regarding?" My mom frowns.

"I'm investigating the release of their client list. Are they a customer of yours?"

My mom shoots a look to me, but the bottom has dropped out of my blood pressure. I press my hands into the counter and try to remain upright. What's going on here?

"I don't know," my mom says. "When would it have been?"

"About four months ago." The police officer checks her notes and nods again.

My mind is grinding, four months ago ... sure, okay, yes, I do remember. A man with three computers and a laptop. I flip back through four months of the certificates, which are written in triplicate, and tear out three.

"Here you are!" I hold them up. "Certificates." I fan them.

"What's this about, officer?" my mom asks.

"Family Planning Clinic has reported the theft of confidential data. They said they recently upgraded their computers and had the old ones shredded. Here."

"It's an abortion clinic, isn't it?" My mom claps her hand over her mouth. "Oh, I feel terrible for those women. This is dreadful."

"We did shred them!" I wave the certificates. "Here's proof. These are the certificates of assured destruction."

I remember, though, the hard drive of the laptop wasn't one of them. The man hadn't paid for that to be shredded, and I'd taken a look through it before sending it out for recycling. Hadn't I? Maybe I'd left it in the drive for a day first, but that shouldn't matter. No one has access to Shadownet except me. Should I tell them about the laptop drive? It was just recycled, not even wiped. I totally remember the laptop because it had a big happy-face sticker on the lid. Our hands are clean.

"Can I have copies of those?" The officer asks.

I jog into the back and run the photocopier. I can barely breathe. Something is very wrong here and I'm beginning to see a pattern. Shivers rattle down my spine, and it's all I can do to keep standing. Before I know it, I've run fifty copies too many, and guilt surges in me about the trees I'm killing. Tears well in my eyes and I clear them before heading back to hand the copies over.

After the officer departs, my mom doesn't leave.

"They were destroyed, weren't they, honey?" she asks.

I can see the disappointment in her eyes.

"Yes! The three computers from the clinic got spaghettified." And it's true, so why do I feel like I'm being hunted?

"All right," she replies.

The door chimes again and I roll my eyes. Cops always have these last-second questions that blow their cases apart. But it's not the cop. The pizza's here. I'm not hungry anymore.

My mother wheels into the back with the pizza in her lap. I lean against the counter, feeling like a kettlebell has landed on my head. I've got my homework for the night and it has nothing to do with school.

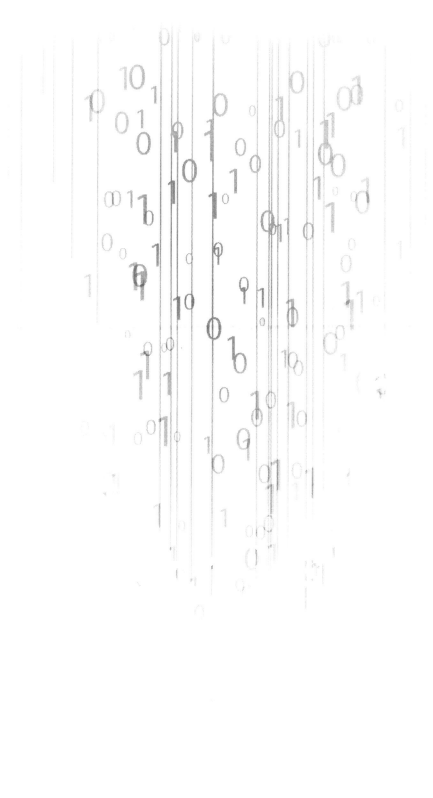

CHAPTER 6

01100100011000010111001001101011011100110110110001101001010110
11100110011101100101011100100010110011011100110010101110100

A FTER COMPLETING MY SHIFT AND dutifully chewing a piece
of cold pizza in front of my mother so she doesn't think
I'm anorexic, I shuffle off to Shadownet. I don't want any
surprises, so I start the proximity alarm on my iPhone and leave
it at the corner of the stairs. The alarm is an app I made using
the built-in microphone to play movie theme songs if anyone
comes by. I enter the basement, my mouth dry. Everything
is humming as always, but the sound of the server no longer
soothes my nerves.

I sit down before my terminal, glance at Jonny's big brown
eyes, and type in my password. It would take an hour just to
sort through all of my emails so I don't even bother, but I do
see *abortion clinic* written in several subject lines; evidently a
couple high school seniors are past clients.

This is bad. With the clinic's laptop long gone, I have no way
of determining if the names came from my network or not.

"Honey!" my mom calls.

Only after this intrusion does my phone play the *Star Wars* theme—I guess there are a few bugs to work out.

"Yes?"

"We made better profit last month, a few more like this one and we can afford the new iPhone."

Any other day I would be doing a Snoopy dance at the prospect of the newest iPhone, but not today. "Cool, Mom," I say, but my tone lacks enthusiasm.

"What are you doing?" A hint of suspicion enters her voice.

"Working on an English essay," I yell back and hope she heard me.

I get down to business, but hesitate with my fingers over the keyboard. What if I'm somehow responsible for all of this? I'm not sure I really want to know for certain.

Family first, I decide.

On Shadownet, Frannie has a live one, an email from Goerge Lewas (his spelling, not mine).

> *To: Frannie Mouthwater*
> *From: Goerge Lewas*
> *Subject: Your WININGS*
> *Dear Mrs. Mouthwater,*
> *I am Director of the UK Lottery Competition and you have one 800,000 pounds!*

Do these things work in real life?

> *Please send you banking information and contact information to unclaimwinnings@UKlottery.cn.*
> *Yours absolutely,*
> *Honourable Goerge Lewas, Director*

So Frannie just has to send all her info to an email address with a .cn extension and collect the money? Doesn't sound suspicious at all! What's *.cn* ... hmmm ... that's China. Now why would the UK lottery have a Chinese email address? Oh, of course, because Hong Kong used to be owned by the UK. That makes perfect sense. Off go Frannie's particulars! LOL.

Heckleena provides a recipe for diced kitten to someone who just lost theirs. She then posts a pic of a cop stuffing Harry into the police car with the comment: *Police bust child porn ring. Child arrested—way to go Ottawa PD #betterthingstodo.*

She's so right—maybe they should be arresting me instead.

Tule follows the real Ellie on Twitter and her tweets are pretty pathetic tonight: *The trip was a surprise for my parent's anniversary, how'd anyone know?*

Woe is me. Evidently the moving service was actually legit. The real thieves paid for the contents of the home to be moved to a storage company, from where it was subsequently removed. Paid cash. The door was open when the movers got there. To me it seems like the real robber was showing off by clearing the place out so well. Who would want people's old paperback books and garage-sale knickknacks? Sure, rob the place, but why go to such extremes? It's like they were trying to send a message, like they knew they had all the time in the world.

I scroll down through Ellie's tweets and find what I am really looking for. I grit my teeth. *Karl helped clean up. His shirt got all clingy with sweat, and he had this man-smell, I know #YUCK, right?*

So not *#yuck.* So, so not yuck. I pull at my shirt, which is feeling a little damp.

In usual Ellie style, the same day she insults me, she asks for help. She's sent me an email asking for a favor. I really can't believe her sometimes. She's such a destructive force, yet so lost when it comes to anything technical.

Can you believe how Hannah made fun of me? I mean, it was so unfair. My only clothes are the dirty ones from Paris. Can you do something funny to this? PLEASE!? she asks. Attached is a picture of Hannah.

Boohoo.

"Paris," I say and shake my head. Amazing how she managed to slip in her travel destination.

If I didn't need to distract myself so badly, I might have told her to go choke on the Eiffel Tower. Perhaps I am inspired by Jonny's artistry, but whatever it is, I pull the image of Hannah into Photoshop and set to work.

I'm self-taught regarding most things technical, but if you ask me, this is the stuff they should be teaching in school. I inspect the picture with an artistic eye, identifying her key features.

I trace around her hair, make a layer, and then apply a filter. Suddenly she has huge, fuzzy hair—check. Balloon pants—check. Let's see if we can't make her a little green—another easy filter application. Something—of course—needs to be coming out of her ears. And why stop there? How about her nose? Eyeballs are for pretty girls, and it only takes using the super awesome bloat tool to inflate her from plump to Stay Puft Marshmallow zombie.

I save the image and reply to Ellie: *Anything for you, Ellie, just don't call me poor again or I'll makeover a photo of you. Just kidding.* Off the image goes! I am not kidding.

The response from Ellie is immediate. *ROFLOL! And sorry I was such a bitch today. <3 Just kidding.*

A cold flush runs through me as I take another look at the new Hannah. The problem with email is that it's so easy to send yet so impossible to get back. I glance at Tule's and Hairy's terminals. I really should be figuring out this Shadownet coincidence, but I also have a chance to rewrite my English essay. I pick up the book and start in on my homework.

The Bell Jar, I discover, is not an easy book to kick off anything for in one night. I read to the word *hullaballoo* and I change the title of my essay to "Hullabaloo" and am pleased.

When it comes to decide whether to use the still-plagiarized *Bell Jar* essay, Gumps thinks, *Time will tell.*

Hairy is staring at me.

Why would you ever send naked pictures to your boyfriend? You just know boys are going to show them around, if not post them to their Facebook accounts when you break up. Anyways, the whole child porn ring is still quite the hullaballoo on Facebook. Evidently while Harry was arrested for distributing child pornography, Astrid was booked for its creation. Which is ridiculous.

It's weird because the Harry I know—and I'm not talking terminal five of Shadownet, featuring Chewbacca as an avatar—Harry would never have shared those pictures. Harry is a smart, quiet kid who runs the chess club. I use his alter ego Hairy to learn about how geeky, late-to-puberty boys think, as well as to play a little chess online without anyone being the wiser. I'm surprised he had a girlfriend at all, let alone one he managed to strip the clothes off of.

A little guilty about the picture I doctored of Hannah, I have the brain surge that I can help Harry and Astrid. After all, Hairy is family and I don't leave my family in the lurch, unlike my father. First I need to determine if those pictures came from Shadownet itself, and if not, then I can discover from where. If I'm at fault, they'd be on his drive. A thrill of excitement shoots through me. I *can* do something.

The essay moved lower on my list of priorities, I kick over to Hairy, whose bushy face growls back at me, and I log in. Regrettably, the easiest way for me to find the pic is to find the Facebook post. I'm not keen on searching for porn.

Unfortunately the picture was removed from Facebook, but I remember the guys talking at school about linking to it. I click through Harry's friends—and I use that term *so* loosely, he has three hundred and twelve (and I bet a hundred of those just wanted to see the pic)—and finally I come upon one that mentions he'd seen the photo on a porn site.

Okay, well there are a million porn sites, but I feel badly for Astrid. Once it's out there, it's gone, there ain't no taking it back. Permanent and distributable. I friend the guy who wrote on Harry's wall and sure enough he accepts me in twenty seconds, becoming his eight hundred and sixty-fourth closest friend. A minute later I'm on his wall and have the link to the porn site. I cringe and click.

There's Astrid with a half dozen other girls, naked. I copy and paste the URL. I'll send it to the cops when this is all over. Astrid is fifteen, this is totally illegal. I also copy the image file and save it. I dig into its properties, learning the file size and type, which is all I need.

I sigh and open Hairy's hard drive.

It doesn't take long. I sort by file type and then by file size.

After a few minutes I hang my head. I find the photo in a folder marked *Love*. Pics, lots of them, but only a few risqué ones. I hit delete, but know that it's way, way too late for that. I don't know what to do? I can't help Harry or Astrid if it makes me look like I'm the one who did it.

The ramifications wash over me with a cold sweat. Someone may have access to Shadownet. What are the alternatives? Harry's computer was hacked months ago and the pictures are only posted now? He did do it? What about Ellie's home break-in and the health clinic's records? This is way too much of a coincidence. I feel violated. I feel. I guess I feel like every one of these people would feel like if they knew they existed on Shadownet.

I suck.

I'm a hack. A crook.

I need to shut Shadownet down and go to the police. Anyone I ever loaded up here could be a future victim. But who is the enemy? Why would they do this to me?

It's already ten o'clock when my mom's voice comes over the shop PA system. "School day tomorrow, Janus."

The proximity alarm goes off—this time it plays the theme music to *Jaws.*

I take a hard look at Shadownet. It's a veritable sinkhole of time. Sometimes I'll sit down for a minute, and two hours will evaporate. I glance over at the image of my mom, looking like she's ready to take flight. An urge to surf through pics of my dad strikes me, pictures of him holding me, hugging my mom, laughing. The need surges so powerfully I'm left drained in its wake.

With my damage done, I climb the stairs to the warehouse and take the elevator up to the offices. The elevator is one of the reasons why we live here. The other being that we can't afford a home.

I lay a big hug across my mom's bony shoulders as she's reading a book and kiss her head. She smiles without looking up. I'm like Judas, hanging my mom out to dry like this. I have to tell her.

"Mom?" I ask.

She glances up from the page.

"I ... uh ..." I think about the guilt trip I laid on her last night and how she's struggling as it is. If I add more of my problems to her, she could crack, worse she could get sick again. Stress is a big factor in MS flare-ups. I recall her look of disappointment when she asked about the clinic's hard drives and don't think I can handle that. I've shouldered a lot so far, maybe I can fix this myself.

"Any dates today I should know about?" I ask instead.

She shakes her head. "You?"

"About a hundred new followers," I say.

"Well if you can't have friends, I suppose worshippers are the next best thing."

I laugh and swallow hard. "Followers, not worshippers, but I guess you're right. Tweeting must be a bit like how a god would feel; you can only really respond to a couple of your followers or you'd get nothing done."

Checking the time, I see that two hours have indeed passed, and my eyes are grainy with sleep. I enter my office and crawl into the big bed, pulling the duvet over my head. Something is nagging me about this crazy day, something I can't quite put my finger on. It's going to have to wait as I drift off into the greatest network of all, my brain at sleep.

CHAPTER 7

01100100011000010111001001101011011100110110110001101001010110
111001100111011001010111001000010111001101110011001010101110100

A NYONE CATCH THE CHESS BATTLE *between grandmasters last night?* Hairy tweets.

@Hairysays Did you actually mean to tweet that? Heckleena replies. *I'm going to whack you with the queen if you don't smarten up.*

@Heckleena they played five hours of genius.

@Hairysays WHACK!

@Hairysays WHACK!

@Hairysays WHACK! Bad pawn.

People are looking at me strangely as I stroll through the atrium, chuckling at the Twitter feed. Looking up, I see that Harry is back and give him a little wave. Yesterday's hullabaloo has died down; if anything, the atrium is quieter than normal. I don't see Astrid, though. Would I go back to school after everyone had seen me naked? The thought brings on a wave of shame as I shuffle to computer science class. Even I had seen her naked and I wonder if that makes me complicit, although

I'm way beyond complicity, aren't I? I might as well have done it myself.

It doesn't help that my backpack feels heavy with my still-forged English essay. I don't have English today, so maybe I'll be able to swing another day's grace if I can avoid Mrs. French (ironic name for an English teacher, I know). It's late morning already, so things are looking up.

"Muh." Chippy groans the greeting like a confused cow as I enter the computer lab.

"Huh," I say back, and he regards me with fat, strangely feminine lips, which he presses together so that they resemble a cat's anus.

I sit at the computer screen farthest from Chippy.

Jonny sits next to me, and I wonder if he does so on purpose, but he isn't looking—his hair cascades in front of his face. I know that doesn't mean much; I look through my hair all the time so no one can tell.

His notebook is beside him, and I let my hair fall over my face so we can both look without looking. Doodles of aliens and patterns in black, red, and blue ink cover the notebook. It's pretty. I want to tell him, but Chippy cuts me off.

"Listen up, everyone, listen up. Calm the self down," he says in a nasal baritone that stops the chatter. "Today we will be making a circle turn into a square using Flash."

I roll my eyes and sigh.

"Do you have a problem, Miss Rose? Muh?"

I shake my head. Transforming a circle into a square is as basic as it gets in Flash. And let's face it, Flash isn't programming; it's graphic design.

"Maybe you would prefer to work in Turing code?"

I shudder at the smirk on his face and shake my head a little more forcefully. Turing code is like putting training wheels on a tricycle, just as useless.

"Good."

I eye Chippy from beneath my veil of hair. He's smiling, and I wonder if he knows about Shadownet. Did he hack in and steal the pics? Maybe I should give the guy a bit more respect. It wouldn't have been easy to crack my firewall. Maybe he's a Black Hat Hacker, a hacker committed to using his powers for evil. Maybe I should look at *everyone* a little more closely.

Jonny tucks his hair behind his ears and fiddles in Flash with various forms of ellipses. I complete the task Chippy set for the class in thirty seconds flat. Jonny looks over at mine and watches it repeat in a loop. I shrug, open a new window, and set about building a small city that will wake with the dawn as the sun rises and cars rumble past. That takes me fifteen minutes.

"Hmm … hmm …," Chippy says as he looks at it blandly and turns to Jonny. "Good, Mr. Shaftsbury." And to me: "Keep it simple, Miss Rose. Try again."

I sigh and show him my first attempt. He squints at me, and I see his hands ball into fists before he nods. "Good, you may leave."

That's the one thing I like about Chippy's classes. If I do it right, he doesn't waste my time.

I pack up and leave close behind Jonny; now seems like a good opportunity to determine what his drawings of me are all about. He's walking quickly, wearing these really ratty, old shoes. One of the soles has peeled back and slaps the floor as he walks. The more I look at him, the more I see how tired his clothes are. Frayed pant cuffs, mended hole in his T-shirt. I think back to his mother with her fox stole and high heels and can't help but hate her a little more. Why was she recycling a three-year-old computer if they're so dirt poor? Maybe Jonny just likes to dress like an urban prophet. Who knows?

"Jonny?" I ask, but he's got earbuds stuck in his ears and is nodding to the music. I jog after him as he pushes through the outer doors. In my peripheral vision I take in the rather large hump of Hannah who cries on a bench. Her hands clench the side of her face. I look from Hannah and back to the escaping Jonny. I run after him, leaving Hannah behind.

As he clears the stairs, Jonny's pace quickens. I already look like an idiot, so I run faster, taking the steps down from the school entrance two at a time. I'm gaining as his hips start to sway like a speed walker's. He stops suddenly and I bowl into him. Lying on the ground, he's got one hand still on the shoelace he'd bent to tie. From one dangling earbud thumps *The Eminem Show*. I love Eminem.

"Sorry," he says.

He's sorry? I swallow.

"Where are you going?" I ask and he looks away. Is he skipping? Maybe he's a smoker. My view of him dims.

His backpack lies on the ground; spray cans have rolled from the open zipper. Cans with white, black, orange, gold, and red caps are scattered over the pavement. I grin at the sight, realizing now why Jonny is wearing ripped clothes. I can make out the paint on them now. He doesn't want to ruin anything.

He just opens his mouth but nothing comes out.

Maybe it's the terrible essay in my backpack that I'm supposed to turn in, or all the drama at school; maybe it's the way his teeth gleam. I don't know, but I blurt: "Can I come?"

Jonny blushes scarlet and his scraggly hair reminds me of one of those shaggy dogs.

"Sure."

I start to reach out to touch his hair, but his eyes widen and I stop. Instead I crawl over to him on my knees and tie his shoe. I kneel with his foot between my thighs, and the world goes silent except for the pounding of blood in my ears. I triple knot the laces to give my heart time to slow. His foot presses into my legs and I don't want to move.

After I stand up, he's recovered too, and we stuff the spray cans back in his pack before walking together, not talking about much. I'm wondering what the hell just happened and my mind's having trouble catching up with what's going on in the rest of my body.

"Harry, eh?" he asks.

"I know, right?"

"Crazy."

"Sad."

"Poor Astrid," he says, and I smile, liking him more. "Do you think Harry did it?"

I clear my throat of the lump of remorse lodging there. "No, can't see him doing that. You like rap?"

"Not really, just Eminem."

"Poetry then."

"Yeah, and a ripping beat."

"And you like drawing," I add.

He flushes red again.

"I mean, I saw your notebook. It's covered."

"If Harry didn't do it, then who hacked Harry's Facebook profile?" he asks. I catch his eye, but can't read his expression. Concerned? Suspicious? How many other people out there are searching for the answer? How many are going to put two and two together and have it equal me? I shrug in response.

We're walking through Brewer Park. Kids slip down slides and monkey about a jungle gym, watched by their parents or nannies. It's cool and I feel fresher and free. I want to check my various profiles and announce on Twitter how amazing it all is, but I resist. Jonny doesn't appear to have a phone even. Decidedly low tech.

"You ever try drawing with a tablet?" I ask.

He shakes his head.

I'd bet he could do amazing things with a tablet.

As we near our destination, he slows to a shuffle as if he's just remembered something and is delaying the inevitable. I know where we're headed: the Underpass. It's this giant concrete canvas for all of the graffiti artists. A legal canvas. I've seen it a couple of times. Each year House of PainT holds a hip–hop competition and these amazing dancers come out and spin on their heads while artists fill the air with paint spray.

I soon find myself walking ahead of him.

"What's up?" I ask over my shoulder. I can't think what Jonny would be regretting in coming here.

"Just not sure I'm totally in the mood to paint today," he says.

I raise my eyebrow. This from the guy who wrote that if he doesn't paint, he'll explode?

"We're already here," I say and jog past the wall of the Underpass. When I see it, I freeze.

There are three stacked layers of graffiti. Each canvas is about as far across as I can reach and as high as I can stand on my toes. All told, forty or fifty wicked murals of signatures, aliens, dragons, cartoons. And one ... one that looks an awful lot like me. Except I'm a cyborg. I've got a camera lens for an eye and these fiber optics sprouting from my head. I look *so* cool. Maybe firewire hair isn't as bad as I thought.

"Sorry, well." He doesn't even try to suggest it wasn't him or that it's not me. He rummages in his pack and pulls a can with a white cap. "I can cover it."

I shake my head. "No, I mean. No!" I yank my phone from my pocket and thumb the camera. "This is amazing."

I snap a picture and then I wave him into the frame. It looks like Cyborg Jan is kissing his cheek but he doesn't notice. Then I dash in and hold the camera out to take a pic of all three of us. I don't have five-foot-long arms so we have to snuggle close to be in the shot and our shoulders are pressed together and the day doesn't feel cool at all despite the damp beneath the bridge and the river running past. I take three more pics than I really need.

"Thanks," I say.

"You want to paint?" He hands over a spray can, and I chuckle.

"Can't be serious," I scoff. The art around me goes from serviceable to *it should be in a museum.* "I draw stick people."

"Why else are you here?"

Why, indeed. Would I be here if I hadn't read his journal?

He takes back the can of paint and reaches into his knapsack to produce a can with a black cap. "So draw stick people." He hands me the new can and points to a spot further down that is just a gray area.

Every month or so a van comes by and paints over all of the art so that it's a new fresh canvas. It's both sad and very Zen, like those monks who create patterns from colored sand which the wind then carries away.

I haven't been frightened for a while, but I am now as I wander up to the big gray spot. I pop the cap off the can and shake it like I see Jonny shaking his, but he's not watching me, he's focused on his own gray spot. I reach out and place a tentative blob in the centre. It starts to drip. And now I have a dripping blob in the middle. I make a sort of circle and pull back a bit so it no longer drips and then ... then I'm painting. And spraying.

Soon my hands are speckled, and I wish I was wearing crappy clothes. The air is redolent with spray paint. I stop thinking of what my mom will say about my best jeans and keep going, stepping back, checking my mural out. Adding a detail here and there.

After a bit I head over and steal some new colors.

Jonny cranes his neck.

"No, wait until I'm done," I say. And he nods. I can't tell what he's doing yet. Looks pretty abstract.

An hour goes by, then another, and I run through the can of yellow I'm using for highlights. Besides the paint, it smells musty in the shadow of the bridge, and cars race above us, thunderous as they pass, but that all fades into the background.

"Okay!" I call, and I don't want to step back to see it until he gets here. When he does, he laughs and I can't tell if it's at me, the art, or something else. His eyes twinkle like his avatar's and I can't believe I never before saw the light in them.

In my picture is this big stick-person head with a wide grin and paint on him like war paint. He's got an oversized paint brush between his teeth and is reaching down with another brush to draw on his missing foot, something I totally copied from my favorite artist.

"Escher," he says and I smile, delighted he caught the reference. The only reason why I know about Escher is because the guy was a mathematician.

"Actually, it's you," I tell him.

"I'm very yellow."

"You with liver disease." I laugh.

"From sucking on too many paint brushes."

"Let me see yours." I dash over while he stands before mine.

I can almost smell the roses and daisies and lilies that twist and dance in Jonny's mural as if they're blown by a warm breeze. In the middle, someone is submerged in a blanket of poppies; a hand reaches to the sky, and from a bouquet of tulips, the tip of a shoe pokes out. I look down. The toe of my shoe.

"Paradise," I whisper.

"What's that?" he asks.

"Paradise," I repeat, staring at his art.

"You're pretty cool."

Heat rushes through me and makes me shiver and rub at

my arms. I check out Jonny, who is leaning back on one leg, hands and elbow crooks full of paint cans and a critical look on his face. In the shadows of the overpass and with the bright sunlight beyond, it feels like we can only see each other, as if it's another world.

He's tagged the bottom of the painting and like all good graffiti it's practically illegible. I finally make it out. *Sorry.* It reads.

I look back to the cyborg, realization dawning on me. The cyborg wasn't a *nice* thing to draw. Jonny was making fun of me. That's why he was reluctant to let me see it. It's why he said sorry when we arrived and offered to cover it.

"Jan," he calls over to me.

I don't answer, but look over.

"Do you want to go out?" he asks.

"Like go to a movie?" I reply.

He's still facing the painting, his Adam's apple bobs.

"Yeah," he says. "A movie."

"You like me?" I glance back at the cyborg.

"I just drew a picture of you," he says. "Of course I do."

So his foxy mother drops off his computer, I steal it, and now he asks me out. Who says crime doesn't pay? But there is the picture of the cyborg. The *sorry.* And my gut telling me that this would be considered ill-gotten gains. Besides, real relationships end badly and the look in his eyes is way too real.

I walk over to him and he doesn't budge, still back on one leg, arms to his side, every muscle flexed.

"Today was really fun," I say, my heart pounding.

He looks away, and all I want to do is reach up and thread my fingers through his woolly hair.

"But ..." he says.

"Yeah," I shrug. "I have to work like every night."

His head bobs and he smiles sheepishly.

"Sure."

"But I'm a really good online friend," I add. I pull my iPhone.

He rummages through his bag and pulls out his phone. I nearly cry with delight when I see it's an iPhone too. Not the latest model, but still.

He holds it out. "Bump?"

And I laugh. We bump phones, which shares our contacts with one another.

At least it's like our phones are going out.

"I'm staying to paint a bit more," he says.

I stand there like a dumb cow before realizing he wants to be alone.

"Right." I dip down and put away the spray cans I used. "I need to go too ... see, ya. Text me."

As I leave the shadows of the Underpass behind, I realize that I do need to head back to school to retrieve my bag.

As I push back the doors into the atrium and navigate the flow of departing students, I'm careful to avoid seeing teachers whose classes I skipped today. I manage as far as my locker. On it is a note:

3:30 PM, Library. Signed, *The Principal.*

My phone says it's 3:35 PM.

CHAPTER 8

0110010001100001011100100110101101110011011011000110100101100
11100110011101100101011100100010110011011100110010101110100

THE LIBRARY IS DARK, BUT not empty.

When I enter, Pig, the school gerbil, suddenly runs super fast around his cage sending pine shavings flying and a shot of fear screaming through my skull. What's this about? I've for sure been caught skipping, but the principal doesn't call students into a meeting for that.

Gray light oozes through the windows as I tiptoe toward a circle of chairs. All are filled, except one. Book dust hangs in the air. Karl looks demure and chews his lower lip. Hannah's eyes are red-rimmed, her face puffy. Ellie has composed herself since yesterday and sits with a straight back, chin high. Principal Wolzowski has his hands clasped before him. A washboard of wrinkles mars the front of his polished bald dome, but whether due to concern, dismay, or surprise, it's tough to tell.

"Good of you to join us," he says.

I bet on dismay.

I look to each of the other students, but their eyes shift to focus on the gum wads stuck to the carpet or on the pattern of ceiling tiles.

"Hi," I say as I sit in the empty chair.

"Who here is familiar with restorative justice?" Wolzowski asks.

No one answers. He cracks his knuckles.

"Restorative justice," he continues, "is an opportunity for the victim to talk to his or her aggressors and for the aggressors to explain themselves. Punishment is determined by the group."

Aggressors and punishment. I'm really not liking this.

"Hannah?" He points to her with an open palm. "The floor is yours."

Hannah looks up and stares at me.

"You're supposed to be my friends," she says, and I'm actually relieved because at least I'm not the only one on trial here and I'm not really her friend, so maybe I'm not in trouble at all. "If I can't feel safe with you," she continues, "then who can I feel safe with? I mean, sending it around was really terrible and I don't know who made it, but still—everyone saw."

I stare at her watering eyes. Oh—this is about the picture I photoshopped of her. Ellie posted it publicly? Of course she did. What else did I think she'd do with it?

"I would like to know who made it as well," Wolzowski says. "Which of you did so?"

His glare lingers on me, and my eyes go to Ellie. She stretches her neck and then yawns.

"All right," he says, "Ellie, why did you post the picture on Facebook?"

"I just thought it was funny," she says. "If I'd known it would upset Hannah so much, I wouldn't have. I'm sorry. It was dumb."

Damn, all the right words, and she even manages a

concerned frown and a small shake of her head as if to say, *What was I thinking?*

"Karl, you tweeted the picture. What do you have to say for yourself?"

He shrugs. "I'm ... uh ... sorry, too, right?"

Wolzowski's raised brow creases further at this, but he continues on. "Janus?"

"What did I do?" I ask.

"What *did* you do?" he replies and glances to Ellie. Has she told him something? Why am I here? If they don't know I made it, and I didn't post it, I did nothing wrong.

"I didn't post it anywhere," I say, testing things.

"Ellie says you forwarded it to her," Wolzowski replies. "She got it from you."

The little bitch. She tattled on me.

"Why'd you do it?" Hannah cries.

I shake my head. "I didn't post it anywhere," I say. "I fool around in Photoshop all the time. Ellie ..." Ellie gives a sharp shake of her head. If I hadn't been looking at her, I wouldn't have caught it.

"Ellie what?" Wolzowski probes.

Does Ellie really expect me to stay quiet after she told on me?

"Ellie asked me to do something funny to the picture. She emailed it to me." Ellie's eyes cast daggers. "In her defense," I continue, "Hannah had said some things that Ellie didn't like that day. I figured it was like giving her a voodoo doll to put pins in. Doesn't really hurt anyone. Ellie shouldn't have posted it."

"But it did hurt someone, Janus." Wolzowski scratches his head as if having difficulty grasping this brave new world of bullying. "What do you think your punishments should be? The best justice is when the punishment fits the crime. Poetic justice."

No one says anything until Hannah puffs out her chest. "I know."

The principal nods at her.

"I want all of us to come up with something beautiful in Photoshop every day for a year and then to share it with everyone on our Facebook and Twitter accounts."

Ellie and Karl both look at me. I bet they couldn't make something beautiful in Photoshop in a year let alone every day.

"Hey," I say. "I'm not about to teach everyone how to—"

"Are you sure, Hannah?" Wolzowski asks. "You want to be a part of it?"

"A team." She brightens. "They all say they take it back, right?"

"How about we make it a hundred beautiful things?" Wolzowski says, but he's not really asking a question. "That seem fair to you, Janus?"

I nod.

"I expect the first tomorrow. It had better be beautiful."

"Beautiful," I repeat and narrow my eyes at Ellie.

As if struck with a sudden burst of energy, Wolzowski shifts to the front of his chair and lifts his hands to us all.

"The next two years will decide your academic future. What appears on your transcripts will be scoured and picked at, and blemishes may cost you entry to your institution of choice. Your future depends on your education. Missteps here could cost. Am I understood?"

Each of us nods in turn.

"Good," he says, launching to his feet.

"Let's get started now!" Hannah's grinning.

"I'm already going to be late for work," I say.

The principal pauses in the doorframe. "Mr. MacLean is still in the computer lab. I'd be happy to call your mother, Janus, and let her know what's happened."

I clench shut my eyes. "Uh ... that won't be necessary, I'll call her." I'm going to be in so much trouble when I get home. I'll lose Shadownet for sure.

"Great!" Hannah bubbles as the library door shuts behind the principal.

Ellie gives Hannah a big hug. "What a wonderful punishment," Ellie says to her, and I can't hold back an explosive sigh.

"Meet you in Chippy's lab in five minutes," Hannah says.

I grit my teeth and return to my locker to grab my bag. To my surprise, Karl is leaning against it. He straightens as I approach, almost as tall as the lockers themselves.

"So you made that picture?" he asks and backs away to give me room to open the locker door.

I shrug and miss my combination.

"You're good at it."

I shrug again.

"I know you think you got a pretty raw deal."

I shrug, the lock snaps open, and I pull my backpack from the depths. He leans over to place a palm on the door next to it. I smell him. Not #yuck.

"Sorry I shared the photo, that probably got you into more trouble. Sometimes I do stuff just because Ellie asks."

I stop, bemused.

"As for this beautiful stuff," he continues. "I can try too. I'm not an idiot."

"Really?" I ask.

He brushes back the white hair that makes him look as though he was struck by lightning. Beneath are those sea-blue eyes. They're smiling and something else. Nervous? Uncertain?

"Not like I'm good, but I can try," he says.

I slam the locker closed. Ellie is hanging out at the end of the hall, trying to hear our conversation. It's past four and I'm already late to take over from Fenwick.

"Give me a chance," he says.

I'm not sure he's talking about Photoshop anymore.

Hannah has joined Ellie and is waving us on.

"Looks like we're a team, right?" I say.

As I walk shoulder to shoulder with Karl, a warm feeling spreads through me. I don't know what's going to happen when my mom hears about this, but there's a definite upside to restorative justice.

CHAPTER 9

0110010001100001011100100110101101011100110110110001101001011100110011001110110010101100100010110110011011100110010101110100

THE STUDENTS FROM THE LIBRARY funnel into the computer lab. I'm nervous; my mom will kill me for being late, but worse will happen if she finds out why.

Hannah bounces in her chair before a computer screen near Chippy's desk. Seeing him causes my heart to sludge into my stomach. I'd hoped I could just kick something off, but with a teacher hovering, I'm going to have to cooperate. We're a team.

Karl rushes ahead of Ellie as if to ensure he sits next to me. Thankfully I don't have to ask for control of the mouse; everyone lets me take the helm. My goal is to be flying out the atrium door in fifteen minutes.

"So," I say. "Let's get this over with."

Chippy looses one of his sick cow, *muuuhhs*. "I'll judge when it is over with, Miss Rose." His breath smells of tuna.

"Something beautiful." Hannah stares at the screen as if an image will magically appear.

Everyone sits in silence for a moment.

"Like a touchdown?" Karl suggests.

"A dew drop," Hannah adds. "A flower bud in Spring."

"Or a baby's hand reaching out of its mother's belly," Ellie says.

We all look at her.

"What?" Her eyes widen. "Like in a C-section ... the doctor is pulling the baby out—" Suddenly everyone breaks into guffaws that leave us gasping.

"I guess that's pretty gross." Ellie chuckles.

"No, no, I've got one—a dog taking a dump?" I say. "A beautiful dog."

"A Praying Mantis eating her mate?" Hannah gets into it, and we're all laughing.

"Zombies eating brains!" Karl shouts.

"What's so funny about zombies?" I ask, serious. Everyone's quiet and then I burst out cackling again.

Muhhh. Chippy doesn't even look up, eyes intent on his work.

It's unclear whether Chippy groaned at us or at what's on his screen. Still giddy, I kick backward and roll to the whiteboard from where I can see his computer. His finger shoots out and hammers the monitor power button. In the flash before he shuts off his screen, I see a glittering website with a rainbow banner. The color scheme alone hurts my eyes. His face scrunches in worry. Chippy clears his throat and delivers a warning glare. I scoot back to the computer a little shaken.

"Where were we ..." I boot up an old version of Photoshop, the humor bled out of me.

"Paris was cool," Ellie says. "The Louvre is gorgeous."

I just nod at the screen thinking about how I'd never left the country let alone flown to Europe.

"Stars, I like stars." Hannah giggles. "The Big Dipper is

my favorite."

Yellow stars had speckled the website on Chippy's screen. I wouldn't be so intrigued if he hadn't reacted so strangely.

I search for stars in Google.

Hannah hums a familiar tune, but I can't place it. Ellie cracks a smile and joins in. When Karl suddenly starts to sing, I nearly fall off my chair.

"Raindrops on roses and whiskers on kittens ..." He belts. My mouth is hanging open which he must take as encouragement because his tenor strengthens. "Bright copper kettles and warm woolen mittens. Brown paper packages tied up with strings. These are a few of my favorite things."

I shake my head in wonderment.

"What, you never see the Sound of Music?" he asks.

"Sure, but I don't go around singing the soundtrack," I say. His voice was clear, strong, beautiful. It's what should be going up on the screen, his voice.

"I know. Let's put the things from the song into a collage," Hannah says.

And it's a good idea, not to mention pretty easy. So I set about collecting mittens and kittens, snowflakes and geese flying in front of a moon. It's weird because I just think of geese as noisy things that crap all over the park, but it's in the song and we're a team.

While I'm at it, I show everyone how to bring a file into the program, cut it out of the original image and paste it somewhere else. It's all really basic but they listen rapt. Chippy eyes me suspiciously, and I bet it's because I'm covering weeks of his material in five minutes. As I'm working I sense Karl leaning in closer and closer. When his bare arm brushes mine it sends a megawatt of long inhibited desire through my bones. My hand with the mouse shoots out and he grabs it.

"Whoa!" he says, giving my fingers a squeeze and guiding

the curser back on to the screen.

I grin.

Ellie's watching Karl's hand.

She coughs hard and bangs her fist on the desk: "This looks like a two year old cut pictures out of a magazine from the forties."

"Did they even have magazines then?" Hannah asks.

"Ask Mr. MacLean," I say.

"Who cares, it still isn't beautiful," Ellie huffs. And I can tell this is about Karl's hand, which he's shifted a million miles away.

"Who cares, it's the idea that counts," I reply, my voice rising.

"I'm not sharing that." She sneers at it and it's too much for me—her expression is too ... French.

"Well, you do it then," I blurt. My chair rolls back a couple of feet when I stand. "Throw in some pictures of your happy family all standing in front of the Eiffel tower wearing berets and stuffing your faces with chocolate croissants."

Chippy is staring. The echo from my screaming fades.

"You're excused," he says.

"What about the something beautiful?" I demand.

"You have done enough for today."

Hannah's chin drops to her chest, while Ellie's tilts toward the ceiling. She slides my chair away and slips hers next to Karl's, taking command of the keyboard.

"Fine." I grab my bag and tramp out.

As I jog to my car, I can't stay grumpy about this ugly *beautiful* project. What a strange day. Laughing, singing, painting and interest from not one, but two, boys?

CHAPTER 10

01100100011000010111001001101011011100110110110001101001011 0
111001100111011001010111001000101110011011100110010101110100

LISTENING TO THE DEATH MARCH, JanusFlyTrap tweets.

Ashes to ashes, Heckleena pipes in before I climb out of the car to face my mother.

My palms are sweaty as I grip the handle to Assured Destruction's door. My mom is going to ask why I'm late, and then I'll have to tell her, and there's no way she'll let me keep Shadownet.

As I open the door, laughter washes over me. The door jangles my arrival, and I cringe.

"Jan? Come and see!" My mom wheels into the store and then spins so fast I worry she's going to roll the chair.

As the door shuts behind me, a clattering rumble fills the front area. Fenwick pushes a huge TV with his pinky and the TV shoots from the store into the warehouse.

"Isn't it great?" my mom says as she chases after it. I haven't seen her so excited since they discovered the whole neck treatment for MS.

A conveyer of silver rollers runs from the retail counter into the cavernous warehouse where the echoes of the TV's passage are starting to fade. At the tail end of the conveyor, in the staging area for the truck, sits the TV. Fenwick beams beside it.

"You're wonderful," my mom says to him, and he gives this odd little bow before delivering his *coup de grace*. The last part of the conveyor detaches, and he pushes it into a cube truck that's backed up to the loading bay. Rolling the TV into the back with one hand, he then cantilevers the conveyor down inside by pulling a pin so that it rocks like a teeter-totter.

"Genius!" my mom calls.

And I admit I'm actually a little jealous I didn't think of it earlier. The conveyor is a holdover from when we used to recycle and needed a disassembly line to sort component parts into bins. It's been lying against the wall for years.

"Careful, Fenwick," I say. "You're going to think your way out of a job."

"Janus," my mom says with a glare.

All the blood has drained from Fenwick's face.

"Sorry, I didn't mean ..." I raise my hands. "It was a joke." Why can I never say the right thing?

"You've got homework?" my mom suggests.

"I'm supposed to cover the front."

"Let me," she says. My mom hasn't run the cash at this hour for a year. I should be happy she's feeling so well, but I can't help but sense I'm being punished and left out.

I let my arms drop and listen to my mom cajole Fenwick into better humor as I head for Shadownet, sorry I broke the spirit of the evening. I inspect the paint covering my hands and smile. Not my spirit. The paint has given me an idea for an app.

I sit down at JanusFlyTrap and start. Apple has made the programming for apps really, really easy. The hard part is creating the design, and I agonize over what a thumb should be able to reach and what not. What happens if the user is left handed versus right. All sorts of things that sound small—and they are, but only if you think of them before you start writing code.

I can't wait to show this to Jonny, but it'll take a while.

I turn on some Feist and I'm counting away, unable to get out of my head how I always think she's going to sing *1, 2, 3, 4, I declare a thumb war*. I start multitasking. Heckleena's Tweeple deserve their heckles. And I want to set up a fake bank website I'll use to trick scammers into thinking they can download Frannie's nonexistent money. If it works, I may be able to lead the police right to the bad guys! At least Shadownet understands me and knows when I'm kidding. I can trust everyone on it not to freak out when I say or do anything. I open an email to Frannie marked *For You* and stop. I shut off the music and read the email again.

I can hear my breathing over the hum of computers.

> *Dear Frannie,*
> *You've been a bad, bad girl. Maybe you should go to the police. What will it take for you to realize how very evil you are? Frannie done a bad thing.*

Frannie has done a bad thing, or are they really talking to me? And who is they?

I print off the email. I check the metadata and already suspect it won't lead me very far. A search of WHOIS leads me to a Japanese server.

Why is someone torturing me? And why would they *want* me to go to the police? Unless they said that to make me question telling the police. Reverse psychology? This is a threat of some sort and maybe I should. But then why didn't I go to the police when I found Harry's pictures on the network? Or when I suspected that the thieves learned of Ellie's family vacation via Shadownet? Now I'm cracking because of an email? Somehow it feels more threatening.

I pick up my phone and dial 9, and then 1, and stop. If I dial another 1, I'm guaranteed to have a police car, a fire truck, and an ambulance here in five minutes. I search for the police department's main line and punch it into the phone. It starts to ring, and I'm ready to ask for Constable Williams, the officer who had stopped by asking questions, when suddenly, I realize what was nagging me last night.

"Ottawa Police Department, how may I direct your call?" a voice asks.

"I ... uh ..."

I can't go to the police. I can't even tell my mom, because she'll go to the police. If we do, my mom will lose her business. Nobody will trust a computer recycler that doesn't destroy its customers' hard drives. Icy cold spreads throughout my groin. I'm alone in this. "Sorry, I made a mistake," I say and hang up.

Suddenly I want to be closer to my mom, and I leave Shadownet and climb the stairs into the apartment. It smells amazing and my mom is not much of a cook. Our kitchen is in the old staff room and the door is shut, but my mom is sitting on our big couch with a glass of wine nearby, her head buried in a book.

"Hi, Mom," I say. "Sorry about Fenwick, I—"

"It's okay," she checks over her shoulder toward the kitchen, then back. "Fenwick's English isn't great and I just waved it off, hoping he didn't understand."

I brighten. It's clear she's still in her good mood. Her hair is piled on top of her head and she's wearing makeup. A half moon of pink lipstick lies against the rim of the glass. Quite the celebration for a conveyor line.

"What happened to your hands?" Her eyes widen; they're green, unlike mine. Mine are so dark that they're almost black.

"Oh." I sit on my hands and lift my legs up so they're sticking out. I love my mom, and although I don't tell her everything, I really do want to share this: "Some boys totally like me."

"A boy did that? To your jeans, too?"

"No, well, yes." I look at the ceiling and see water marks—repair needed, more money. "He's a graffiti artist and he let me do some painting on a wall."

"He's a vandal?"

"No!" Argh. "It's a graffiti wall. A legal one."

"So how do you know he's not a gangster?"

"Because we live in Ottawa, okay, Mom? The most boring, not cool city in all of Canada. The place fun forgot. And we're not even dating or anything so don't worry about it."

I can tell she's biting back another comment. There's a knocking coming from the kitchen. It sounds like someone is chopping something.

"Is someone here?" I ask. We haven't had company in months. Not since my aunt came over for Easter. Months. Unless I count my mom's secret dates. A date!

"I've met a boy, too," she says and then blushes.

"What? A man?" I should have known. The food smells, the kitchen noise, the makeup, the wine. I check the wine to see how much she's had. I know she likes wine, but she can never finish a bottle so never opens one.

"Don't seem so surprised." She cocks her head.

"I know I shouldn't be after our conversation but to actually have another man over in our house ..." I don't know why, but I don't like this. Not with everything that's going wrong right now. "Who is he?"

"You can meet him yourself."

The kitchen door is open, and the fluorescent lights inside

silhouette his tall frame. He picks up a tray and strides toward us, features becoming clearer as he nears. Gray hair, face slightly mottled with age, but a strong jaw. His eyes are a little watery.

"You said you'd met a *boy*," I whisper.

My mom's arm sweeps over and whacks my shoulder. If she could have, I bet she would have kicked my shin.

"Peter." She pauses and shows teeth. "I'd like to introduce my daughter, Janus."

He puts a platter of steaming dumplings in front of my mom and takes my hand. His is cool and clammy, and I don't like holding it.

"Hello, Janus." His voice resonates in a rich baritone. "I've heard a lot about you."

"Pleasure," I say and slump down to put my hands back under my thighs. "So, where'd you two meet?"

And there goes my mom, blushing again.

"I told you, the Internet, honey." She takes a sip of wine. "It's not like I get out much."

This guy could be a predator. I've heard stories—geez—I'm in the middle of one! I eye him more closely. I suppose that if she's gone gaga over some geriatric, it's my job to play the role of parent and be suspicious. Peter's wearing several gold rings, one with a big ruby. Like a lot of old people, he's dressed too well for the event and has on a neat suit and tie. My mom is way too young for him. It isn't right. Worse. It's gross.

"The Internet. That's interesting," I say. "You must know a lot about each other then."

The air has been sucked out of the room. It's a bell jar.

Neither can tell if I'm being facetious, and I feel like a third wheel. But I can't help but think that this is a car accident waiting to happen. What should I do? Be a bitch and ruin the night? My mom doesn't get out, it's true. So maybe I should just let it go.

"Actually, this is our third date," my mom says.

I release a long breath. The two lovebirds share a look. How gross!

"Please." Peter holds up the dumpling platter and smiles. I can't tell if his teeth are dentures or not. I take a dumpling, and they're really good even if it's not pizza. My phone is buzzing (it's always buzzing) and I use it as an excuse to flee back to work.

I take the exit stairs instead of the elevator, punching through the door at the bottom so it slams hard against the wall. In the dark, the emergency light glows red and the roller line glints. I go to the window and peer out at a nice-looking, powder blue Mercedes. I try to think like my mom. We need money so she finds an old guy who won't be around too long? A year ago I would have done anything to support the family. Maybe I'm driving her to this by demanding fewer work hours? My stomach twists. Powder blue. I mean, who gets a Mercedes in that color?

I can't decide if I don't like my mom dating online, or dating at all. The only obvious thing to do is find out who the heck he is. I wander down to Shadownet, comforted by my network of friends.

I click away the image of my healthy mom and bring up an old picture of my dad. In it, he's holding out his hand, face earnest, as if beckoning me to follow.

"She's moving on, dad," I say in a warning.

I slump into my chair and suddenly realize I don't have Peter's last name, Googling *Peter* won't help. I don't feel like creating anything beautiful either, so instead complete my ritual of updating everyone's walls, feeds, and blogs.

Is ten too young for a boyfriend? Frannie tweets the world.

Ten is too young for Twitter. And tweeting for boyfriends is never a good idea, Paradise57 says.

Oh come on @paradise57says, I want to see what happens to @Franniemouth, Heckleena replies.

NO! JanusFlyTrap tweets. *I won't let anyone else get hurt!*

And it's so weird because there are tears in my eyes as I send off an imaginary tweet to protect imaginary friends.

I wipe my eyes and inspect Frannie's spam folder. She has another ream of it, and I scan through carefully to see if I'd missed any other threats. At the last second, I catch a weird email. It's a comment notification like I receive when someone comments on my blog posts—an email saying someone left a comment. But Frannie doesn't have a blog. Who is commenting on a nonexistent blog?

Other notifications I missed are scattered amongst the hundreds of spam emails. I let out a small whine and click on the link. There it is: the mystery site. Except, it's not a mystery; I recognize it.

CHAPTER 11

THE WEBSITE GLITTERS WITH LEPRECHAUNS and pixies that dance on rainbows, hearts, and stars. It's like a box of Lucky Charms barfed on my screen. It's the same site Chippy had up on his monitor this afternoon. I'm positive.

Everything is in shades of pink and purple, including the barely decipherable text. I highlight the whole thing and doing so makes the font legible. A series of short topics have been posted, and everything is anonymous, including comments— at least, that's how it appears at first. The blog posts are in hot pink and the most popular as measured by comment count are:

Who does she think she is?

What do you get when you cross a donut, a dog, and a fart?

And:

Why doesn't she just die?

I suspect that I don't want to read any of the responses but I click the donut-dog-fart post anyway. Beneath are seventeen answers. I check Frannie's spam folder and sure enough I find all seventeen comment notifications. Looks like the site went live at some point last night, and people were commenting the whole time I just happened to have skipped class. Coincidence? I'm choking on coincidences.

The answers are pretty juvenile—*well if she's a princess then I'm the pea*; *queen of 0110001001101001011101000110001 101101000* (I translate—BITCH—points for the use of binary); *I actually think she knows she's pathetic*; and so on.

It's not a pretty picture and it's clear who they're talking about. Evidently when you cross a donut, a dog, and a fart, you get *me*. And as to why I don't just die—because that's me too ...

Yeah, I know, right?

Or: *Maybe she already is dead.*

And: *Maybe she's a cyborg.*

The last one leaves me cold. The sender is Anonymous—they all are—but what's the chance of Jonny painting the cyborg and then someone mentioning it here? Maybe I'm over-thinking. I don't know what to think. All it would mean is that Jonny is on the site, not that he created it. I hug my knees to my chest and wrap my arms around them. Why wouldn't he warn me? Maybe he's embarrassed about my rejecting him again and he's taking an anonymous pot shot.

If I'm receiving notifications, it means I have the keys to this thing. I search through Fanny's mail but can't track down the password into the blogging platform administration. Somehow Chippy, or whoever set it up, has the comments coming to me, but without giving administrative access to the blog. All I can do is comment. I could complain to the host, but I have to decide if I really care.

Why doesn't she just die?

I rub the gooseflesh on my forearms. That Chippy could be my tormentor is a relief. Otherwise the guy who posted the topic ... Or girl, I guess—I'd rather get punched in the face personally than crap like this—someone may want me dead.

A chill climbs each vertebra of my spine. My hand hurts, and I realize I've been gripping the mouse so hard my knuckles are white. I release and flex my fingers. My iPhone starts bleeping away with notifications, but I ignore them. Nothing can be more important than the website.

The code I write next is gobbledygook for the average citizen, but to me it's genius. Or at least, a good idea. When it's ready, I prepare a comment of my own.

What do you get when you cross a donut, dog and fart, you ask? It's amazing that my opportunity to take my revenge on Ellie has occurred so soon. I upload a link to a picture of her with the offending code I just wrote imbedded in it. I'm banking on the fact that whoever created this site is eagerly waiting to click on people's new comments. I'll delete evidence of my reply as soon as I know who is doing this to me. If it's Ellie, then so much the better.

I don't have to wait long. Someone—Anonymous—replies: *Not cool. She's awesome.* And I know I have them.

The code attached to the picture was a piece of malware. A small .exe file. A trojan that should—any minute now—open the address book of the victim's computer and send me an email. And there it is in Frannie's inbox.

From: Ellie Wise

A small thrill snakes through me. Then the thrill turns icy.

This all of course makes perfect sense if Ellie knew anything about technology, but I suppose she could set up a blog.

Someone writes another post about me, but I ignore it. I have another hit on the Ellie pic.

From: Bob MacLean

I clench my head between my palms. Chippy!

I can't ignore the coincidence. His reaction to my seeing his screen. The site he was looking at—I'm sure it was the same one. If I'm planning to take on a teacher though, I need proof.

I unfurl, delete evidence of my initial reply, and start writing a new bit of code. This will be a little more complicated. This time the code will hide on the victim's machine and wait for me to activate it so I can take a peak around. That part's easy as long as I know the IP address, but creating a trojan like this won't be simple—

Oh no! What the ...

Beside me, Hairy's computer goes blue. I cry out. Blue is worse than dark. Dark means no power. Blue means there's something wrong with the operating system or the hard drive. They don't call it the Blue Screen of Death for nothing. What's worse, the timing can't be an accident.

I type faster. These are my friends, my family. I've spent weeks rebuilding and months creating them.

Frannie goes blue. My heart rams against my ribs. I have to make a decision: Save the hard drives or get this code up? My dad. My mom. Everything could be lost.

I dive for the wires.

JanusFlyTrap's blue ... good excuse for my essay? No one will buy it. I pull the first plug. Heckleena's gone. Tule's gone. I tear all the plugs from their seatings in the powerbar. On the ground, I clutch them like a bouquet of flowers. It's too late. My image of my dad beckoning blinks away. The only plug I yanked in time was Paradise57. My hands and knees press into the concrete floor. It's possible that this is just a system error and I can recover all my files, but if this was targeted, then everything could be gone and all I'd have left are memories.

Gumps is still flashing green at me. Of course—he's not connected to the Internet. Nothing could have infected him. I still hear a humming and slap my forehead: the backup server. I sprint to it, but just as I arrive, it shuts down all by itself.

I shriek. And crumple to the floor, where I sob.

A minute later, my iPhone proximity alarm goes off—I really need to delete it from the app store, makes me look bad. But when I wipe my eyes, I see Peter at the base of the stairs, watery eyes now clear.

"Quite the network you have here," he says.

I bite my lip. "Had here. Something just shut me down."

"Virus?"

I shake my head. "There is no way a virus could have gotten in. I'm so careful."

"Sorry to hear that, Janus." He looks uncomfortable. "We heard the scream ... and your mom can't, well, you know."

"I know."

"Not that that is important," he adds. I look at him weirdly, not inclined to be nice to anyone tonight and failing to care that my view of him might be important. If I just got nailed with a worm, why should I let him off the hook? "I'd prefer she could walk, of course," he says, fumbling around for the right words. "Your mother is very special to me."

Special is such a loaded term. If someone called me special in school, I'd flip out. So I say, "Great, my mom must think you're special, too."

He looks at his feet. "You're okay, then?"

"Yeah, thanks."

And as he walks back up the stairs, I realize that now another someone can access my private space. I don't like it. Not while my mother's business is at stake. Not with her heart on the line.

I plug Hairy back in and try rebooting. On the screen blinks the message to please install the operating system. I shut the computer back down and sidle over to Gumps. *8-ball question: Is Peter using his money to date my mom?*

Response: *Outlook not good.*

I stare at the dark screens. The only light is from the green phosphorescence of Gump's monitor and the occasionally bleeping iPhone, full of Facebook notifications.

I cry and wonder what to do. I can't bring myself to see how bad the damage is on Shadownet. I dread school tomorrow. I don't want to go upstairs and be around Peter. Shadownet is mortally wounded. I pull my sweater over my head and huddle against the cooling server.

CHAPTER 12

0110010001100001011100100011010110111001101101100011010010110
1110011001110110010101110010000101110011011100110010101110100

I HUNKER DOWN IN THE FRONT seat of my car in the school parking lot. As I wait for the bell, the tape deck (you heard right) is playing one of my mom's old The Who tapes: *Who are you? Who, who, who who.* I'm avoiding everyone. I don't want to hear the rumors. The snide remarks. I now know why I have a hundred Facebook notifications. Someone impersonated me and posted the link to the blog on my own page. Another space of mine hacked, and I use pretty strong passwords. At least I'd thought so.

@JFlyTrap You're kinda like a boulder rolling down a mountain causing an avalanche that crushes all the innocents in a village, aren't ya? Heckleena tweets.

It's not your fault @JFlyTrap, it's the bad peoples', Frannie replies.

Would any of it have happened if not for @JFlyTrap? Hairy asks.

No more Facebook, no more Twitter, no blogging, I'm offline,

JanusFlyTrap tweets.

Who are you? Give us back our @JFlyTrap! Heckleena demands.

"We'll see how long it lasts," I say aloud. The bell rings and I kick open the car door.

English is my first class. I run from my car to the classroom. Despite my best efforts to avoid people, I still catch whispers as I jog through the hallway.

In class, my teacher stands at the white board, surveying the few stragglers.

"Please place late essays in the pile at the front."

I open my mouth to protest, to tell her that my computer crashed, then the server, and that someone is maliciously targeting me, but it all sounds crazed. Janus the computer nerd loses her data? Besides, it doesn't matter. My mom said, "Pass your courses or bye-bye computers." Well, Shadownet is offline. The only thing I can do is send tweets and posts over my iPhone and respond to email. It's like Shadownet has arms and legs, but no heart.

It's ironic that my backpack holds the only copy of my essay—if you don't count where it came from. I reach inside and leave "Hullabaloo" with the few other late essays, including Karl's; he smiles at me as I lay mine on top of his. After I sit, I concentrate on them as hard as I can, but unfortunately they don't spontaneously combust.

I don't take English with Jonny, so instead I spend the class doodling about him and Karl. I can't participate in the class discussion because they're going over what the essay should have contained and I haven't read the book beyond a Wikipedia plot summary. Instead, I draw Jonny brandishing a huge paint brush and Karl wielding a baseball bat. They duel until Jonny sticks the paintbrush into Karl's eye socket, but in a final swing of the bat, Karl wallops Jonny in the side of his head staving in his skull. By the end of class, they're both bleeding out on the ground, dying for their love of me.

"Janus, the principal would like to speak with you."

I look up. Mrs. French's lips are pursed. Class is over. I'm one of a half-dozen kids lingering. I'm not worried about the principal; I can guess what he wants to talk about. I shrug my courier bag over my shoulder and walk out. When I reach the offices, the school admin assistant waves me behind the desk.

Chippy is leaving the office ahead of me. My concern ratchets higher, but then, maybe he has been caught. The school takes bullying seriously.

I knock on the door.

"Enter."

I turn the knob and walk into the room. My breath catches in my throat. It takes a lot to force my mom to drive, and here she is, sitting on the principal's big couch.

"Mom?"

She stares at me. The principal points to the couch with its free seat right next to the police officer, the same one who came poking around Assured Destruction about the health clinic. Constable Williams.

"Hello, Janus," she says. "I'm with the cyber crime unit in the police force."

I clear my throat without saying hello.

"Are you familiar with a website where anonymous posters are making comments about other students, including you?" the principal asks.

I nod.

"It's quite clever of you, Janus." He smiles and grunts appreciatively.

I look to my mom in confusion, but she's giving nothing away. Stone faced.

Principal Wolzowski checks a file and then shuts it. "We know you're intelligent, but you're failing several courses, including computer science."

I start in, but my mom cuts me off.

"No, Janus," she says. "Listen."

"It's come to our attention that you created the website that allows anonymous respondents to make posts and reply to posts regarding other students. Including one that suggests a student die."

"But—" In my head I'm screaming, *I die*. It suggests I die.

This time it's Wolzowski who holds up his hand. "Someone posted a picture of Ellie Wise and inserted a piece of malicious code, a virus that takes over the computer creating what Chipp—what Mr. MacLean calls a zombie and uses the inbox to propagate—"

"It sends an email, one email," I blurt.

My mom looks at me and shakes her head. I've just handed the principal all the proof he needs.

"I didn't make the website," I add. "Mr. MacLean did. I saw him surfing it yesterday."

"We find that hard to believe. Mr. MacLean brought the site to our attention when he realized it dealt with Hopewell students. That only occurred when you posted Ellie's picture. We think you made yourself the focus to distract people from its real purpose."

My mind is whirling ... how convenient of Mr. MacLean to tell them about the site. It keeps his hands clean.

"Janus," my mom begins with a warning glare to not interrupt, "when the principal called, I was worried for you. I had Rogers Communications take down the site and track the IP addresses of the users to see if any used its services. It did. A Frannie Mouthwater. Does that name ring any bells? Because all of the mail is going to that account. It *is* yours, isn't it? It's the same name you gave one of your dolls when you were little. The one that vomits when you squeeze it."

"I don't know how to explain," I say. And I don't. Not without getting into Shadownet and confiding that I've been stealing the hard drives of customers. Maybe if the cop wasn't here, I would have told, but she's wearing handcuffs and a sidearm.

"I bet you don't." There's sarcasm in my mom's tone, which hurts more than anything that's been said so far. "Your relationship with Ellie Wise is no secret, dear. Just because she told on you about this Hannah incident doesn't give you the right to—" She cuts herself off, red faced and head shaking.

So she knows about Hannah—great. It was dumb of me to use Ellie's picture; I really should know better. Wolzowski opens his mouth to speak, and I feel like a ball being kicked around the school yard. "This site could have done a lot of damage, Janus. Ellie Wise is not happy, but luckily it appears the only person you have really hurt is yourself. She's not going to press charges." He nods at the constable. "This time."

I lower my chin. If I did tell them about everything else, I'm not sure it would help. And this has grown very personal. Chippy, or not, I will find out who is doing this to me and I will destroy them.

"Given that you don't appear to have learned your lesson from yesterday, and considering there isn't even anything beautiful in my inbox due to your altercation with Ellie. I have no other option but to suspend you until further notice." The principal folds his hands on the desk. He passes the ball.

"And grounded," my mom says. She shoots—"*And* you will still send something beautiful to the principal every morning"— and scores. So much for the team.

The meeting ends with a lot of dark glowering. I'm escorted by my mother through the hallways. We stop at my locker and I collect the rest of my books. Teachers will send on homework via email. I spy Jonny at the end of the hall and I don't know what to do. His hair is back in a short ponytail. I give him a pained expression, but I'm sure I just look constipated.

"Help me," I mouth, but don't know if he catches it.

"I'll see you at home." My mom pushes the button to open the atrium door and rolls smoothly outside and down the ramp. We'll be driving home separately. It'll be my last few minutes of freedom. I turn back for Jonny, but he's gone.

Would I have had my face pressed up against the window?

I shake my head and stroll to the parking lot, balancing the stack of books in my arms. I open the trunk of the car, let loose the landslide of books, and flop my bag on top. Once I'm sitting in the front seat, I heave a sigh.

"Can I come?"

I cry out, and Jonny's head pops up from the back seat.

"Sorry," he says. "I guessed where you would be headed and had to hide when a teacher walked past. The door was unlocked ..."

"Yeah, I'm not too worried about someone stealing the sound system." I twist in my seat. "What are you doing here?"

"When a friend of mine says *help me*, I help."

I nearly break into tears. I'm not much of a weeper, and here I am, twice in twenty-four hours. He reaches out and touches my shoulder.

"You better go," I say. "Here comes another teacher."

"I'll walk back from your place." He ducks. "Drive."

I start the car and ease out of the parking lot. Once moving I keep well below the posted speed limit, wanting the drive to last as long as possible.

"So what's happening?" comes the disembodied voice.

And I make the decision to tell him. To tell him everything. It feels so good to offload the guilt, the fear, the confusion, to have someone I can trust who knows. The only thing I don't mention is that I've been poking around in his hard drive—that would end our budding relationship and I'm not ready for that.

After I'm done, there's nothing but silence in the back for a full minute.

"So what you're saying is that you're taking people's private files and using them to recreate them online?"

"Yes."

"And now someone is targeting the real people behind the profiles?"

"You got it. And me, I think the real target is me," I add.

I can't see his expression, but I can tell he isn't too impressed.

"How could you think this whole thing was a good idea?"

"I—listen; I'm not the one attacking them! Okay?" My voice cracks, and his head bobs up.

"Why *do* you need imaginary friends?" he asks.

"Whoever is attacking Shadownet isn't imaginary, and the people he's hurting *aren't* imaginary."

We're almost at Assured Destruction and I don't want to end our conversation on a sour note.

"Maybe you should think about that?" he says.

If he hadn't phrased it as a question, I might have blown up, but he had. "I have. I do care," I say. "But if I go to the cops, my mom will lose the business and we'll be on the street."

He's quiet again for a moment. "So, Ellie has been hit. Harry. This clinic. You with the website. Who does that leave on this Shadownet?" he asks.

I swallow, annoyed with myself that I hadn't considered who might be next. "Gumps, who is dead—but that computer doesn't count, it's pre–Web. Heckleena, who was one of my first, and Frannie, who would be twelve or thirteen by now."

"Are they okay? Do you think it might be one of them?" There's a pause. "That would make sense. I'd be pissed if you turned me into one of your Internet minions. That would give motivation."

I bite my lip. The fierce look in his eyes tells me that he'd throw me to the wolves if he knew he was part of Shadownet. Here he is, skipping class and walking back four miles in order to have this brainstorming session, and I can't tell him the whole truth. I like Jonny, but I always feel guilty around him.

"Chippy has motivation too," I say.

"Yeah, but you have no proof."

"I could hack his computer ..."

"If you think you're in trouble now, try breaking into a teacher's files," he sniggers. "Geez, you're a magnet for this stuff."

"All right, the other Shadownet profiles at least give me something to focus on." I pull into a parking spot well away from the front entry and turn the engine off. My mom's van, thankfully empty, is parked at the other side.

"This isn't good," Jonny says. "You need help."

I agree with him, but don't know what to say.

"Why didn't you tell me about the website?" I ask. He looks surprised. "I could tell you were on it once you downloaded Ellie's picture."

"Oh, right," he says. "I'm no good with computers. I didn't know the site was about you. You're the one who posted the link on Facebook. Why would you do that if the site was about you?"

"But that wasn't me, that was just someone who hacked my account!"

"I know that now, but didn't last night," he says and opens the side door. "Be careful. Someone is out to get you."

"Jonny?" I say, and he pauses. "Come see me later? Just send a text and I'll let you in back. No one's downstairs after eight o'clock but me."

He nods and skulks off to the side of the parking lot before circling back.

"It's not like a date," I say to myself.

CHAPTER 13

01100100011000010111001001101011011100110110110001101001011011
1110011001110110010101110010001011100110111001100101011101
00

NSIDE FENWICK IS MANNING THE cash, and he smiles at me as I enter, showing three gold teeth and shakes my hand like I've just won the kettlebell championship. Seeing him reminds me of my mother's business problems; she would have had to call him in to cover for her, and that takes money. Normally she takes care of the cash until lunch since we get so few customers.

I'm about to head downstairs to start rebuilding my network when Fenwick starts to stutter something, waving his hand around as he searches for the right words.

"Mother tell *up, up*." He points.

I take the elevator to delay the lecture another sixty seconds.

The doors open on the second floor, and my mom waits for me in her chair next to the couch.

"Sit down," she says.

I sit on the armchair, as far away as possible.

For the next minute she stares at me. I've never seen my mom so disappointed.

"Your comparing Ellie Wise to a donut, a dog, and a fart is unacceptable." I try not to laugh, hearing my mom say fart. "And you made fun of another girl the day before? What am I to do with you?" Tears well in her eyes, and my smirk crumbles.

"What do you mean, Mom?"

"You! You're so smart, but you're failing. You don't try. I *am* giving you too many hours at work. I can take some more, or maybe Fenwick ..." She trails off and I know we can't afford more Fenwick. "Your courses matter. How you perform will decide if you earn scholarships. I don't know if a scholarship is even possible now—suspension." She unclasps her hands and stares at them.

I know she's right, too. I need a scholarship if I'm going to continue my education, or I need to make a lot of money fast. But all of this. Almost all of it. Can be cleared up if I hunt down who is doing all the nasty business and drag it into the light. It's probably some other kid, and we don't even need to bring the police into it. Hopefully tracking down the people behind Heckleena and Frannie will provide clues. For now, I have to take my punishment in order to protect my mom.

"I'll do better, Mom. I can't explain how I'm going to fix all of this, but I am."

She eyes me. "It's not just school. You were rude to Peter last night."

This I don't have to take. "Come on, Mom, how can I take him seriously? He's ancient."

My mom draws a breath and releases it before continuing. "He's an accomplished man, who is handsome, and good to me. I'm not asking you to think of him as a father."

"Right, because he could be your father," I say.

"Janus, whom I date is my business and I can't ask you to like him, but you will be pleasant to him." She folds her hands away into her lap.

"I'm your daughter, Mom, so it is my business and I don't understand it, okay?" I really do want to figure out her relationship. I need some way to ask for his last name without raising suspicions.

"You will understand when you reach my age." She says this as if it'll end the matter.

"You mean, if I need money? Because that's all I can see. That you need his money."

She pauses; tears streak her cheeks. "I'm." She draws another sharp breath. "I'm not a ... not a whore."

"I didn't say whore!" I shoot forward and clutch her hands, but she pulls away.

"Get out of here, Janus." She points to the stairs. "Just leave."

Holy crap, what have I done? She's turned in her chair and is wheeling for the kitchen. To be as far away from me as possible.

"I—"

"Out!" She keeps wheeling and slams the kitchen door behind.

I shuffle to the exit, slipping down each step of the stairs.

"It go good you?" Fenwick grins when I reach the store.

"No, Fenwick, not good for me," I say. "Why don't you go home?"

He frowns and looks at his watch.

"Just go," I say. "Sorry, please, just go."

He looks back twice more at the stairwell, and I realize I'm taking money out of his pocket by forcing him to go home. I don't care, he can have his pay. I just want to be alone until I can face my broken Shadownet. Finally he leaves, and without another word, which isn't like him.

The day's quiet as a graveyard. I have a chance to check my mom's computer, which seems fine. I'll fix the server tonight and make a copy of her files just in case. A customer drops off an old IBM ThinkPad that seems in decent shape. I decide to refurbish it. It's not that I haven't learned my lesson; I just want to connect to the Internet using something that isn't infected.

The laptop's missing the power cord, and I find a candidate in a box in the basement. I promise myself that I'm not going to look at any of the files and boot it up. It's old enough that it doesn't have a WiFi card, but I have some old ones around. Twenty minutes later I'm on the Web. My forehead relaxes and my face smoothes. On the Web I'm in my element, even though someone is swimming in my territory. The browser is frustratingly slow, but I can begin to search.

Frannie Mouthwater's real name was Stephanie Meeps. Meeps is not a common name, I hope, but I doubt she has much of an Internet presence given her journal is filled with unicorns and rainbows. Her father is a David Meeps; her mother, Helen Meeps. Their digital fingerprints were all over her computer as I suspect it was theirs at the outset.

Since Frannie would only be about twelve, I search for David Meeps first. I still get thousands of hits and add LinkedIn as a key word. LinkedIn is a social network for business types and I recall that David was some sort of numbers guy—accountant, I'm guessing. I find eight Meeps on LinkedIn, two in finance and only one relatively local—looks like they moved to Montreal, a big city about an hour and a half east of here. He doesn't blog or have a website, but I can see that he works for Naylar and I could call him and ask if Stephanie's all right. How normal would that be? He's linked to his wife, which makes life easy for me. She's a nurse at a Montreal area hospital. She too has no website or social network that I can track down for updates on her daughter.

Without any luck so far, I type in Stephanie Meeps, but don't expect much from Google. There's an eighteen-year-old punk rocker named Meeps, but nothing younger. This Meeps has enough piercings to be on the cover of the next *Hell Raiser* movie. Definitely not my gal. I keep searching, but Punk Meeps overwhelms the search results. Just for the hell of it, I friend her on Facebook, then swallow hard at the notification badges littering my own wall. On my Facebook profile, I've got a ton of comments and have lost a couple hundred friends.

Your profile is hacked again.

Everyone defriend her! This from Hannah; I guess I deserve it.

My mom saw your message, thanks a lot.

UR Hacked!

Loooseeerrrr!

Screw you.

Nice pic!

My profile pic shows a donkey; Chippy is taunting me with the same picture I put up on his blog! But I can't use that as evidence either; I'd have to admit I hacked him first. I'd changed my password this morning, so whomever it is has managed to figure it out a second time.

About half the notes are from haters, the other half from people trying to help me out. The damage is done. I change my password—something I should evidently do hourly—and post a general notice.

So, so sorry. I've been hacked again, anything you've received from me in the last twenty-four hours didn't come from me.

I see a post from Karl.

Hey everyone, this is obviously not Jan anymore, so please stop saying mean things to her. Thanks, Karl! Of course, he has ten comments, all telling him off.

Back on Meeps's page, I see I can "like" her and I do, bringing up her fan page.

Hometown: Ottawa.

Huh. I'm sort of let down. The computer must have been older than I had thought. All this time *my* Frannie has been a goodie two-shoes, and now I see that in reality she's a hardcore rocker. Moreover, the real Meeps is probably a lot more interesting than my Frannie. The computer must have been lying around for five years before they got rid of it. Meeps has a blog and I click through.

Blackmailed! it announces. Turns out that those journals that were so cute and cuddly and heart-warming are now dead weight. A fetish for unicorns and rainbows is good if you're a children's author but not an asset when fans prefer you to have a thing for tattoos and fishnet stockings. She's laughing it off, but clearly someone tried. Pictures of gutted unicorns and colorless rainbows are strewn over the blog to prove her point. I will have to download myself some Meeps music.

With an attack on Meeps confirmed, but no real damage done, I turn my attention to Heckleena's forerunner. There's a reason why Heckleena was my first. Much like Roz Shaftsbury, she was this bitchy woman who walked in, demanding she be served first and left in a huff when I wouldn't, dropping the computer where she stood and walking out. But not before saying, and I quote:

"I should have just tossed it in the garbage. Try to do something right and the peons will stop you at every turn."

She called me a peon. With my mom bedridden, a line of customers to service, and a week's homework to do, she called me a peon. Heckleena was born.

Her real name is Aina Ehrstrom and if I recall correctly she didn't have a job that I could find. Ottawa's home to a lot of government workers (one of the reasons why it's so boring), and I always suspected she was in government. I try searching for her, but Ehrstrom is common enough that I don't get decent results. I add search terms for Ottawa and government and have one hit. A photo of a dozen people from a society party. Beside her is Andrew Ehrstrom, ambassador to Canada from Finland. In a quick search I see he's ambassador no longer. Aina isn't on the continent. I feel sorry for the peons of Finland.

With my concerns over Aina and Meeps allayed, I log in to my Apple developer account and work on Jonny's app. Three more customers interrupt my coding, but all in all a decent day, and I even manage to forget about what I said to my mom until I hit the intercom to see if she wants pizza for dinner.

"No," she says coolly. "Peter's cooking tonight. He doesn't do pizza."

Another nail in his soon-to-be needed coffin. Who doesn't like pizza? Suddenly, I see my chance to learn his last name.

"No Italian blood in him, I guess." I'm trying to act casual, but it's sounding a bit forced. "I mean, what's his heritage anyways?"

"What are you talking about?" My mom's voice is deeply suspicious and a little confused.

"Just saying, he looks like a Bergmann or a MacNeil rather than a Michelangelo." I swallow hard.

"Moore—it's Welsh I think," she replies.

"That makes sense, the Welsh hate pizza. Okay, bye!"

I hang up. I finally have Peter's last name, but *Moore* sounds way too common. I Google it to be sure and come up with thirteen million hits. Peter Moore in Ottawa is little better at ten million pages. To buy any sort of credit report I'll need his address and social insurance number. That won't be easy.

I check my email, actually hoping a teacher has sent me homework, but there's nothing from school. But there's an email from Karl. I hold my breath as I click through.

The subject line reads *We support you ...* The body of the email continues: *Everyone knows you're awesome at tech stuff, but I'm totally amazed by you being a hacker. You have to teach me some day. One day we're all going to be working for you. SUSPENDED, that's cool. Annoying, I bet, but cool.*

Of course, I'm happy but—he likes me because I'm a

suspended hacker? Boys are messed. And who's *we?* I'm betting Ellie and that sucks the romance out of the email. He's also asked me out to the movies, to which I reply that, unfortunately, it may be cool to not have to go to school, but I'm also grounded for the foreseeable future.

On Frannie's account, my torturer has vanished. She's won a new car, another lottery, she needs to act FAST on an investment opportunity, and must update her MasterCard information, but somehow the fun has gone out of it. The real Meeps shoves her head into mine, and I can't pull off the innocence Frannie used to have. Heckleena's still a class-one bitch but I don't have anything mean left to say. I said it all to my mom earlier.

A certain pastel Mercedes pulls into the lot, fishtailing in the gravel. Peter hops out carrying a bag of groceries and a bouquet of roses.

"Hi ya, Janus!" he says.

I muster a smile. "Hello, Peter."

"I'm sorry to hear you're having some trouble at school." He shifts from foot to foot, and I can't tell if he's really sorry.

"I'll work it out, say—" I add. "What do you do?" I glance at his Mercedes.

He grins. "I like to golf, play bridge—"

"For work?"

"I'm retired, Janus."

"And before that? What was your job?"

He studies me for a minute. "I was a consultant."

He's not making this easy. "Of what?"

"Your mom didn't tell you?" he asks, showing me all his possibly fake teeth like he knows something. "I figured with all the problems you were having she would have mentioned that I worked in the computer industry. Internet security."

My jaw nearly falls off when it unhinges.

"She didn't?" He stops shifting. I think his surprise is genuine but I can't read his eyes.

I shake my head.

"Well, maybe we do have some stuff in common." If he looked happy before, he now seems to float as he wanders into the elevator.

Something Jonny said in the car reminds me. Whoever is doing this needs a motivation, whether it's Ellie's for my liking Karl, or Chippy's for the attacks on his website. Just then I figure out Peter's motivation. My mom has been dating him for at least a week or two and old people have lots of time. If he knows computers, then he's had plenty of chances to hack me. What if he wants me to go to the police so that my mom loses her business—loses her business and falls right into a certain wealthy lover's protective arms?

CHAPTER 14

0110010001100001011100100110101101110011011101100011010010110
1110011001110110010101110010000101110011011100110010101110100

THERE'S AN OLD MOVIE CALLED *Fatal Attraction* that my mom let me watch when I was too young to see it. In one scene, this psycho chick cooks the family's pet bunny rabbit. All afternoon I picture Peter cooking rabbit for dinner.

Luckily dinner is fish. But I hate fish. At least, I hate fish skin and fish bones, and the fish head Peter lops off with the glinting cleaver—and the clear suggestion that it could be used to cleave the head from my neck too. At least that's what I assume; I didn't even know we had a cleaver. It freaks me out that his first step toward moving in would be to bring a knife and not a toothbrush.

Sitting at the dinner table across from Peter, I eat the fish but only because I hadn't dared venture back upstairs for lunch and am near starving.

"Do you want the cheeks?" Peter asks.

"What?" I reply.

My mom nudges my arm with her elbow.

"*Pardon*, Janus, the word is *pardon*." My mother slumps further in her chair. Normally she gets into a real chair for meals, but tonight she just rolled up to the table as if she couldn't be bothered.

"Pardon?" I try.

"The fish cheeks," Peter says, "are a delicacy and only given to the most honored guest in Chinese culture."

He offers up a small piece of meat. The gelatinous eye of the fish accuses me. I imagine it saying—no, not my cheeks. I need my cheeks to make fishy faces.

"I, ah, no thanks. You're the guest." Although I feel more like an outsider every day.

He shrugs and places it on my mother's plate.

For a moment the only sound is of our cutlery. Fragrant dill and lemon scent the air.

"When was your first date?" I ask and they both pause mid-fork stab.

"Why?" my mom asks, eyeing me.

"No reason, just wondering," I say.

"Would have been a week or so ago? Maybe eight days?" Peter looks to my mom for confirmation and then back to me. "Why don't you tell me what happened to your network."

I tense. Is this like when a serial killer returns to the scene of the crime to glory in people's reactions to his dirty work?

"Janus?" My mom prods.

I fail to see the harm in explaining the symptoms. "I've got a ring network attached to a server. They all went blue screen."

"All at once or one after the other?"

"One after the other."

"Firewall?" he asks.

"Yup."

"Updated antivirus." He waves it off, and together we say, "Overrated." And I laugh despite myself.

"So what do you think?" he asks.

"I don't know. I don't download much."

"What about something you didn't download, something you brought in on a memory stick from school?"

Right—or a hard drive. I shake my head, but inside I'm screeching. It makes perfect sense that the trojan came from a hard drive, but my most recent acquisition is Jonny's. Did I manage to unplug the network before the virus got to Paradise57? Or did the virus come from it? Just when I think I've figured out my enemy, I find another clue.

I barely make it through dinner being civil. I want to return to the ruins of Shadownet. Of course my mom can read my mind, and she raises her sing-song voice as I clear all the dishes and scrape the scraps into the waste bin.

"No more computers, Janus."

I go cold. She has no idea what's at stake. I can't be banned from computers, not now.

"I need it, Mom." I try to keep the fear from my voice.

"For what? People lived quite well before Facebook and Twitter."

"Homework. I have homework assignments."

"And we have a library with lots of books and you have a library card."

I stifle a laugh. Homework using books? What is she thinking? She's gone mad. I need an excuse, a foolproof one. *I'm working on an app* isn't going to cut it. *I need to talk to my potential boyfriends* won't either.

"Hard to do computer science homework without a computer," Peter says lightly.

We both whirl on him.

My mom turns slowly back to me, and I wipe the look of desperate appreciation from my face.

"And do you have computer science homework?" she

demands with one eyebrow arched.

"Some," I say. "I am failing."

"Thirty minutes a day. That's it. For homework."

She checks her watch as if to say *starting now*. And I sprint for the stairs. I ignore the muted argument behind me, figuring that if Peter's the bad guy, he'd want me on the computer. The jury's out on him.

I land in my rolly chair and walk it over to Jonny's terminal. I disconnect everything except for the power supply and boot up. I don't know what to think when it loads perfectly. Paradise57's luminous eyes sparkle at me.

My suspicions are high. I start to inspect. Trojans like to change the registry keys so they can restart your system without you around. They usually attach themselves to programs you use a lot like a web browser. That way, when you start the browser it starts the trojan program too. I run a virus scan and it comes back clean. I figured that, though. This code was specially written for me.

It takes the full thirty minutes for me to find the odd registry keys. I don't bother trying to clean it out as it's guaranteed to be hidden in more than one spot. This guy is good. It's not worth my time. I've found what I've come for. My mom calls out. My time is up.

What hurts the most is whose computer the trojan is on: Paradise57's. It came from Jonny's hard drive.

My mom calls again. "Now you're losing tomorrow's time."

I swear and pick up my iPhone, only to see that I've missed a text from Jonny. He's outside. I freeze. I just found out he or his mom is my torturer. Good. Maybe I can put this behind me.

I jog upstairs to the warehouse and kick open the back door. It's dark and cool out. A light rain is falling.

"Jonny?" I whisper.

A cat scoots past the entry; I clap a palm over my mouth to

keep from crying out.

Boots on gravel, and then he's here, wearing a sodden, black hoody. It'd be funny and cute if I wasn't ready to accuse him of sabotage. But when I try, I can't say the words. If I do, and I am wrong, I lose a friend. And I have very few friends. My mom calls again.

"I have to go," I say.

His eyes flash from disappointment to anger. "I've been out here almost half an hour." His teeth are chattering. If I wasn't so suspicious I'd hug him, or I'd let him inside and he could leave after he'd warmed. But, I don't trust him. Not now. Not when he might have brought a trojan into Shadownet.

"Does your mom like me?" I ask.

He seems to darken beneath the hood. "She's kind of overprotective," he says finally. "She wouldn't like that I'm here, if that's what you mean."

What I mean is maybe she doesn't like me and she's setting me up to hate her son. This is nuts.

"Did you find out about Heckleena and Frannie?" he asks, wiping water from his eyebrows.

"They're okay," I say.

He starts rubbing his arms. My heart breaks a little and I wave him inside. "Just for a minute."

"Thanks." He bounces up and down and smells wet and cold. I bite my lip and shudder when he draws me close. I tense in his arms.

"I'm sorry this happened," he says.

He says sorry a lot, but never has anything to really be sorry for, unless maybe he has a guilty conscience. He might be cold, but his lips feel hot on my neck and send white lightning down my spine.

My mom's next shout is insistent. The kind that says *just because I'm in a wheelchair doesn't mean I won't come and get you.*

I don't want to go anymore.

He presses his lips against mine and we kiss for a moment, fingers threaded together. It feels like I'm making out with the enemy—like I'll come home sometime and find him cooking the cats. I stop and realize that I'm not really kissing back.

"I have to—" I begin.

He doesn't wait for me to finish.

"Jan—" He shakes his head. "You know I've liked you for a while ... and you invited me here." I nod, remembering how he asked me out and that it wasn't all that long ago that I thought of him as stalker. "So, *do* you like me?"

I want so badly to say the right thing. I even open my mouth, but all that's racing around in my head is that I've determined why he'd do this to me. He's angry for my rebuffing him the first time.

He grunts as he breaks my grip and tugs his hoody tighter. In a dozen steps, he disappears into the night and rain. The door slams shut.

Slowly I start to walk away, but then I remember to feed the cats. I open the door again. And gasp.

Karl is staring at me with a mixture of annoyance and uncertainty, white hair plastered on his face and blue eyes shining. In his arms is a fat gray cat.

"I thought he'd never leave," he says.

"Karl!" I say. "What are you doing here?"

He steps inside, puts the cat on the steps, and lets the door shut behind him. He's only wearing a T-shirt, now soaked and sticking tight to his muscles.

"I want to talk to you," he says. "I felt terrible that you were stuck at ..." He glances around the warehouse interior. "... here. What did Jonny-boy want?"

The whirr of the elevator starts as it climbs up to our

living room.

"Crap, my mom is coming. Wait right over there." I point to the deepest shadows and then run for the exit, climbing the stairs and hoping to beat the elevator. I push into the living area as the elevator car arrives. My mom is halfway into the elevator and backs out.

"Mom," I say. "I just need ten more minutes."

"No," she replies, her stare icy.

"I forgot about something beautiful. You said I need to make something beautiful every day. I forgot."

She eyes me. Peter is on the couch and offers me a wink.

"Ten minutes," she says as the elevator doors *whomp* shut. I race back downstairs.

"I only have five minutes," I say to Karl, "but I really do have to make something in Photoshop while we talk."

Karl leaves wet footprints as he follows me into the bowels of the warehouse. I'm chilled now, and after I sit in my chair, he leans in over my back and places his hands on my shoulders.

"Why do you have a cartoon on your computer?" he asks as I click away from Jonny's caricature as quickly as possible. Should I tell him about Jonny and me? Is there a Jonny? If I do, then I'll lose all chance with Karl.

"I'm crazy, okay?" I crane my neck. He's looking out at all the blank computer screens. "Why did you come?"

His fingers begin to massage my shoulders and slip down over them, inching toward my chest. I lean forward, only granting him access to back. The fingers keep working, and it feels good.

"I told you," he says, "to work on something beautiful." His hands massage a little harder to ensure I catch his drift. Strong fingers peel back the stress in my muscles.

I flush and tap away on the keyboard for a minute before realizing that I'm not connected to the Internet. I swallow as I bring up the only pictures I have to work with—graffiti.

"You like this stuff?" Karl asks with a note of surprise in his voice.

"Yeah," I say. "I like it a lot."

I choose a mural of a woman dancing on top of water; she seems as light as dandelion fluff. Then I import it into Photoshop and add text: LIFE IS BEAUTIFUL. Satisfied, I connect the printer and then hit print so I can prove to my mom that I did something. Karl's fingers are edging close to my breasts again, one hand swooping down. I catch his palm and hold it.

"Sorry, Karl," I say. "I really have to go."

He grips my hand, spins the chair, and pulls me up and into him. He presses his lips against mine and we linger for a moment before I pull away. Jonny would apologize at this point, but not Karl. He smiles like a Viking with a chick over his shoulder.

"Maybe once you're done your suspension," he says.

I swallow and draw him up the stairs by the hand. At the backdoor, I hold it open as he steps out into the rain, feet dancing through the puddles as he jogs away.

CHAPTER 15

01100100011000010111001001101011011100110110110001101001011 011100110011011011001010110011000100010111001101110011001010111010100

LIFE SUCKS THEN YOU DIE, Heckleena tweets. *Except me, I will live on in Twitter.*

Even Twitter will die one day, Hairy says.

@Hairysays Sacrilege! Heckleena replies.

I send these as I stand, bored, in the Assured Destruction store. It's morning and I know what I have to do. Today I will eliminate Jonny as a prospective boyfriend and quite possibly uncover the identity of my nemesis. But I can't enact my plan immediately. I have to take my mother's shift until Fenwick arrives, at which point I'm supposed to do homework at the library.

My mom may be limiting my computer time, but she doesn't know about the ThinkPad. After the Jonny and Karl tag-team event last night, I couldn't sleep. I spent most of the wee hours under a blanket, working on my iPhone app. Even if Jonny's a crook, it's a cool app, and I finally got it finished around four o'clock and sent it off to Apple for approval.

This morning, I discover that *Life Is Beautiful* has been passed around the Facebook walls like wildfire. Maybe it's not such a bad punishment after all. But even with being able to tweet and Facebook, I still spend three hours twiddling thumbs until Fenwick arrives, then I pack up and make like I'm heading out to do my schoolwork.

"I'm leaving for the library, Mom." What I really need is a nap as I grab the car keys from the dining room table.

"And you need to take the car to get to the library?"

It's around the corner. I freeze mid-step toward the stairwell. "I … I'm so used to going to school I guess." I toss the keys back.

Her brow rises, but she doesn't say anything. Close one.

I fly down the stairs and run to the back of the warehouse to grab my bike. Biking will cost me time.

At the nearest Starbucks I borrow their WiFi—I don't have enough money to pay the coffee-rent and my iPhone isn't great for hardcore Web research. Using my laptop and the 411 directory, I discover that there are three Shaftsburys living within a ten-mile ride of the school. I check the school catchment areas and rule out one of the families as living outside of the borders. With only pedal power this is going to take longer than I'd hoped, but I still have a couple of hours before Jonny would typically return home from school. I can do this. I slip the laptop into my backpack and swing on to the bike.

Soon I'm sweating and my palms are slippery on the handlebars. I'm sure this is supposed to be good for me, but as salt burns my eyes, I can't see how. I turn on a busy street and climb a long steady hill. I pedal for another fifteen minutes. Sweat's running down my back in rivers, and I catch the bike chain on my jeans three times before I pull over to the curb. I look around and don't recognize a thing. I punch the address into the Google Maps app. It helps take me from A to B in the form of a flashing blue dot and highlighted path. I hug my phone to my chest.

Not seeing anyone I know around, I bend down and cringe as I wrap my white athletic sock over my already oily pant cuff. I'm a dork, but I refuse to wreck my second pair of jeans in a week. I set off pedaling again.

The blue dot finally connects with the Shaftsbury's address pin. Their home is on a quiet residential street with older houses from the twenties, the yards dotted with large oaks and maples. Nice—not poor—middle class with some low-rent housing mixed in. I cycle right past the house as I don't want to raise suspicions. The porch is clean and newly painted. Bright yellow shutters stand out against red brick. No car in the cobblestone driveway. Nice.

I cross the street and circle back, stopping in front to lean my bike against the rugged bark of an oak tree. Brown and orange leaves crunch beneath the tires. My first job is to confirm I've got the right place.

Mail sticks out from the mail slot. I look around casually and then jog up the porch steps. Without knocking, I check a letter. *Mr. and Mrs. Michael Shaftsbury*. This gets my feminist goat and doesn't help. The next letter provides my answer. Ms. Aliana Shaftsbury.

I'm actually relieved it's the wrong house.

"Excuse me?"

A woman on the sidewalk squints up the steps. She and a two-year-old stand between the house and my bike.

"Aliana?" I ask, mind whirling.

"No," she says. "I'm a neighbor."

"Do you know when she gets back?" I keep everything light. I'm supposed to be here. No need for police. You've seen me before. On your way. Move along now.

"Usually five, who are you? Reading mail is a felony."

My Jedi mind tricks clearly aren't up to par.

"Can you tell her Iva Goddago stopped by, please?" I ignore her comment about felonies. People are so over dramatic. Really? Are all mail carriers felons then? It's a wonder any mail makes it to the right place.

She doesn't say anything, and I waltz past her and her kid, stopping to say, "Well hello there, cutie-pie." And then I'm off.

As I turn the corner, I start laughing and laugh so hard I have to stop and clear my eyes or risk whacking into a parked car. My phone buzzes again and I check it. A tweet to Heckleena telling her off—one of many. But it's weird: *What happened to you?* It appears someone has hacked her Twitter account and is sending out nice, syrupy tweets worthy of a greeting card on Valentine's Day.

I'll love you until the day after forever.

When you see a falling star tonight, make a wish, it will come true because I wished and I found you.

Holy crap, *I* even hate her.

I don't have time for this, but it reminds me of my plan. I punch in the address for the next Shaftsbury and start pedaling. My thighs are already burning and my butt feels like I've sat far too long on something way too pointy. The next house is on the other side of a really big triangle, and it takes a good half hour to reach. Factoring in time to bike home, I have maybe twenty minutes on site to do what I need to do.

As I approach the address, I skip the drive-by. I let the bike fall against the sidewalk and rip the laptop from my backpack. The home is a pre—war job. Semi-detached, squat, ugly, aluminum sided with a single-car drive and a carport. The garden in front is well tended and the lawn trimmed.

I don't even bother checking the mailbox. I don't have time—this is either Jonny's house or I'm too late. I sit on the curb, buttocks rebelling from the cold, hard concrete, and boot up the ThinkPad, which is grindingly slow.

Breaking into a wireless network isn't all that hard if you know what you're doing. I loaded the hard drive with the programs I need, and the old wireless card is actually handy for this job. Unfortunately I'm not using Linux, and so this makes placing the wireless card in monitor mode a little trickier. This is all blah-blah-blah to most people but it costs time. Basically, by using some special software, I can collect data that allows me to figure out the password with another piece of software.

I don't collect as many packets of data as I'd like, so the second piece of software—AirCrack—takes a lot longer than I had hoped. Still, I penetrate the wireless network within six minutes and only one car has driven past.

After that it's a cinch to find Jonny's computer—there are only two on the network. I wonder if I should look at his or the other one.

A door slams behind me, but it barely registers.

I'd rather rule Jonny out than his mother, so I choose Jonny's. I need to be able to trust someone in case this starts to get really dangerous. A cold fist in my stomach is telling me it already is. I see he has a webcam. I could hack it if I wanted to and look around his room. Sick, right?

Instead of totally violating his privacy, I find his Firefox web-browsing history and pull it up.

"Hello?"

The question is to my back. At the familiar tone of the voice, I almost wonder if the last Shaftsbury's neighbor followed me here. I flip the lid of the laptop down.

"What are you doing?" she asks.

This woman is overweight and wearing a large floral print dress with black tights underneath. Another big yellow flower sticks out of her hair. Her gut sticks out at me.

If it worked once, it'll work twice, so I give it a whirl.

"I'm, ah, looking for Roz Shaftsbury."

The woman lifts a drawn-on eyebrow. "Are you?"

"Yeah, I—" I pause, hoping she'll come out with another comment but she doesn't, only bringing a ham fist to her hip. "She's not here so I'll come back."

"No, she's here all right." She smirks. "You're looking at her. Now what do you want?"

I'm stunned. Unless Foxy Lady ate herself five times, this is NOT Roz Shaftsbury, not the one who dropped off Jonny's computer.

"Mom? Jan?" Jonny's walking down the sidewalk. He's home early. Then I remember—computer science class is last today. Chippy lets you out early if you're done. "Why are you at my house?"

"Who is this?" His mom asks him.

I need to run or I'll be late for my shift. My head's whirling.

"What are you doing here, Jan?" Jonny asks.

I'm realizing that something really bad is going on. If this isn't Roz, if this isn't some petty revenge taken too far, if this is a conspiracy, I'm in way over my head.

"I didn't like how we ended last night," I say.

"Well, maybe there shouldn't be a *we*," Jonny states. "If there ever was."

He's still mad—I would be, too. And he doesn't know about Karl.

"Can I talk to you, Jonny?" I ask. His mother's eyes narrow as I've lowered my voice. "It's about the Shadownet."

His lips are thinner than I remember, eyes a dull matte.

We walk a little ways down the sidewalk. "I have your old computer," I say.

"What?" And a sudden light flashes in his eyes as if he's hoping for a rational explanation. "You took it?"

"I didn't take it. Some woman dropped it off at Assured Destruction, even asked for it to be destroyed, but she said her name was Roz Shaftsbury and I wanted to see if it was your computer." I speak so fast I'm not quite sure what I'm saying.

"How'd you know it is mine?"

"Your files."

"You went through all my stuff?"

I cock my head.

"You shouldn't be looking through people's private stuff!" he says. "Wait." He points at his mom, but I know he's talking to me. "Why are you really here?"

The question's loud enough for the street to hear.

"I caught her with her laptop open." His mom scuffs the curb with her slipper.

"You thought I was the person doing this to you." Not a question. "You were hacking our network." Jonny's eyes fly wide with hurt.

"Shh ... I just wanted to see if it was your mom."

"But it's not my mom, and I won't *shh*. Someone very bad could have all my personal stuff and I don't know why."

"They're after me," I say, but I know he's right. Someone had taken the trouble to find another student's computer and ensure it landed in my hands by impersonating his mother. This is bigger than me, and Jonny knows it.

"Really? Because you haven't had someone steal naked pictures of you, or had your medical history shared, or *anything* except that stupid website that you probably *did* create."

I lower my gaze and my throat constricts. Everything is starting to make sense—why Jonny's journal entries are all three months old and why there were no pictures of Foxy Lady on his hard drive. He has nothing to do with any of it. His laptop and Foxy were the true trojans.

"Am I one of your digital slaves?" he demands. I back up a

step, but don't answer. "Am I?" He grips my shirt and twists it into his fist. "I saw *Life Is Beautiful*. Funny thing, I took a picture just like that."

"What's this about, Jonny?" His mom stomps toward us.

I shake my head and say in a hush: "Don't tell, give me a week and then I'll go to the cops."

He looks down at his fist and opens his fingers, letting my shirt go slack.

He seems to consider this—the Underpass feels so long ago. "Twenty-four hours," he says. "Then I call the police myself."

"Forty-eight hours," I plea. "I need a friend, please."

"This time tomorrow." His voice is even and cold. "And if you want any more help, maybe you should talk to whoever I am on your stupid network."

I can hear his mom's huffs nearing, but I'm staring into Jonny's dark eyes. He knows I don't even have fake friends anymore.

"I'm sorry," I say. And then I scramble around Jonny's mom, grab my pack, and race off on my bike.

As I pedal, I hear Jonny say, "Don't worry, Mom, she's a freak."

My tears aren't of laughter this time as I turn the corner, and I'm still upset when I pull into Assured Destruction, sweating, disheveled, and out of breath. My mom's at the cash. I'm fifteen minutes late. I stand at the door, mother grimly watching from inside. And just when everything seems dark, I catch a glint. A flash of hope.

Sunlight reflecting from the lens of our security camera.

CHAPTER 16

01100100011000010111001001101011011100110110110001101001011011001100111011001010111001000101110011011100110001010111010100

I WAIT, SWEATING IN THE ENTRY of Assured Destruction. Inside, it's cool and dark as my eyes adjust. My mom's shoulders are back and her jaw flexed. Slowly I roll my bike to the wall and lean the frame against it. Her sighs whistle from her nostrils.

"Where were you?" she demands.

I can't tell her what I've really been doing, but I can't lie to her anymore. "I went to a boy's house."

Her chin tilts down so that now she's looking at me like a wolf might when ready to pounce.

"It's complicated," I add with a sniff.

Her expression suggests she's considering whether to lock me in a closet or to hug me close, but something else is wrong. Her mouth opens and closes, and she frowns. I've never seen the vein at her temple throb so prominently.

"Your school called," she says. "They're deliberating your expulsion."

I stand nonplussed, wracking my brain for what new terrible

deed I have committed.

"Why would you do it?" she cries. "What are you going to do if you are expelled?" Both my mom's hands are in the air like she wants to karate chop something.

"I haven't done anything, have I?"

"Are you this mixed up?" she asks, face screwing in confusion. "How can you not remember plagiarizing?"

"Plagiarizing ..." And then I catch on. OMG. The essay. I wouldn't have thought it possible for me to get into more trouble.

"No, no I remember, but—" I set my bag down slowly, like I'm placing a gun on the floor under threat of death. "I just didn't have time to finish the essay."

"Because of your computers."

"No—well—yes, sort of," I begin and sag. "Listen, Mom, I need to tell you about everything that's happening, but I can't. You'll understand why when I've fixed it."

She rolls her chair back and forth. I've seen her do this before. She's thinking, weighing the options.

"Maybe you need some help," she says. "Maybe I can help you."

And this is why I think my mom is so cool. Here I am, a cyberbully, a plagiarist, a liar, and a jerk to someone she cares about, and still she's there for me. I begin to cry.

"I'm really sorry it's gotten out of control. I'm losing friends because of it too." I sob.

"What got out of control? What's going on?"

"I can't explain yet. I would if I could."

"And you will," she says quietly. Anger is not far off. "And until you do, you will go from here to the library, where you will check in with me, and then you will return and you will work. That is all. You will rewrite that essay tonight and hand it in to me at midnight."

"Then I need my computer," I say, wiping my eyes.

Her face pinches. "Why should I trust you?"

I swallow hard. I'm sixteen. My mom is treating me like I'm six. "You can't. You shouldn't. I'm a lost cause." My tone is sincere.

"But I want to trust you." Her voice cracks. "So I will."

She turns slowly in her chair, only using one hand, with the other at her temple. I realize that I just used reverse psychology on my mother. Her heart is in my hands.

"Take over for me, please," she says, and I can't believe how much I've hurt my mom. "Peter's coming, ask him to come back tomorrow."

She wheels into the elevator before I say anything in reply.

I wait and the doors close with a thump. The sadness wells in me; my mom, my failures, my hurting Jonny and Hannah, Harry, Astrid. My lungs hitch and my mouth turns down; another choking sob escapes my chest. With its echoes I'm overcome by grief and I'm on my knees, tears dripping from my elbows as they run from my hands and down my forearms.

After a few minutes, I rub my eyes and run fingers through grimy, sweaty hair. The cry has cleared my head and strengthened my resolve. All my pain, and everyone's vengeance, hinges on me solving this mystery. My expulsion. Mom's business. A boyfriend. Justice for Harry and Astrid. Even for Ellie. I need to set this to rights. I climb to my feet and head for my mom's office.

The office is a room with no windows, two filing cabinets, no chair, one desk, and a shelf at the same height as the desk so that my mom can reach everything. We keep security video tapes on a seven-day rolling basis, so we have tape from a week ago, which we'll soon copy over. The images are grainy, but enough to identify a person or car or—if I'm lucky—a license plate.

I pick the tape for three days ago and plug it into the display unit. It goes all crazy with snow and then returns with an image of our parking lot just in front of the door on a sunny day. The time stamp is 8:04 AM, which is when we switch the tapes. Then it goes black. I rewind it well past halfway, trying to recall when Foxy Lady came in. It takes another minute of searching to catch the snarling eyes peering into the camera lens, but the car is parked out of view and a lens flare obscures some of the frame. I pause the tape and start to rewind to see if I can catch the car as it comes in. I do; it's a Honda Civic, black, but there's no plate on the front. I try for the rear as it leaves.

The door jangles, and at first I think it's the tape, but there's no audio on it.

"Dear?" a man asks.

Who says *dear?*

Peter! I pause the video and scramble out of the office. Peter stands at the cash, on the threshold of crossing over into the *Employee Only* area.

"Hi, Peter," I say. Instead of a bouquet of flowers, he's holding a pizza box with a hard drive on top. On most days I'd be impressed that he's carrying my two favorite things in the world. Today I need to get rid of him. "My mom's really upset— because of me—and asked you to come back tomorrow."

His face crumbles, and I can see how upset he is. On the other hand I still believe he is a retired dude who likely has too much time on his hands. He's probably planning on taking my mom on an all-you-can-eat cruise as we speak. I quell my evil thoughts and try to like him.

"It's not you, I swear, we just had a huge fight," I say. "She needs a long time after a fight; she's always been like that."

"Can I leave these with you?" He proffers the pizza and hard drive with a hurt smile.

"What's the hard drive for?" I ask.

"It's mine. Destruction, please."

I hold it tight in my white-knuckled grip. It's my chance to rule this guy out. It's my opportunity to unearth who this man really is. There could be souvenirs from past killings on it. Records of his fraudulent activities. Or, better yet, evidence of his plans to destroy me. I owe it to my mom to search it.

"Assured," I say.

He stands, looking from the drive to me to Chop-chop. I can tell he's torn between wanting to make a good impression on me and wanting to see the thing shredded into strings of metal.

"Don't worry, no charge," I say.

He pauses for another moment, makes some sort of decision, and smiles thinly before letting the door jangle behind him. The drive still feels hot in my hand as if it's just come out of a computer. I've been here before: A tempting hard drive, one with something potentially malicious onboard.

After his Mercedes exits the parking lot in a swirl of dust, I slip the hard drive into my backpack for later and sprint into the office. The screen is paused with a view of the lot and the nose of a Honda Civic at the bottom edge of the frame. I move the video forward frame by frame until I have the rear of the car. And I've got it: Foxy Lady's license plate.

It's too late in the day for phase two of my plan. I feel like a runner peaking for a big race. Twenty-two hours remain between now and when my life shatters into a million tiny pieces.

I can't leave the cash for a while yet, so I do something I should have done weeks ago. I fetch *The Bell Jar* from downstairs and crack the spine.

I read the first page and my knee starts to shake, jouncing the book. I flex my leg muscles to make the tremor stop. Then I take a look around for customers and run my hands over the conveyor rollers as I devour page two. The rollers make a fun sound, especially when I spin them back and forth. I set the book down and see how many I can keep rolling at once. Fourteen. I read another page and have the urge to pee.

I admit it; I have a problem. I have the attention span of a gnat with ADHD after six cups of coffee. Forget for a moment that a gnat wouldn't drink coffee. Here I am, only about seven pages in, and my mind drifts toward the hard drive and what secrets reside there. I snap back to the book for a few more pages and I learn how this chick Esther gets this wicked job at a fashion magazine and instead of being like—whohoo! Woot! Woot! Woot!—she's like, *whatever*. Then I'm back ogling the hard drive and am pretty sure that I can beat my record of fourteen rollers.

I have to figure out a way to keep my attention focused on the book. Six hours remain before I need to hand the essay in, and for some reason that deadline seems almost as important as Jonny's. While balancing a slice of pizza on my fingers, I boot up the laptop.

I have an idea. If I can spend hours going back and forth between Twitter accounts, blogging, and Facebook, why can't I use Shadownet's accounts to write my essay? I mean, I'll just let each of my Shadownet characters respond to one another and they'll write my essay for me?

I start by logging into a half dozen accounts. Everything has been hacked and is messed beyond belief but I don't care. I know the voice of the characters and this is a good idea. Besides I'm not sure I care as much about these people anymore, they don't seem as real as they once had. All I know is that between them I've written over ten thousand tweets, and if you figure ten words a tweet, that's one hundred thousand words, which is a book. I CAN write an essay across social networks.

Heckleena pipes in that she thinks Esther is a head case. Esther isn't engaged by the New York fashion scene because she's totally depressed. Frannie wonders why Esther never recognizes herself in any photos, or even in the mirror.

I don't have Gumps alongside me, but I can imagine what he'd say to that, so I type into a new Word document: *Who you are is what you see.* Or don't see, I guess. And that sounds smart even if it isn't totally clear.

I keep working like this, reading—there's even sex in this thing! Way to go, Mrs. French—and having the characters comment. The hours tick by and Esther leaves New York and becomes trapped in the suburbs—the symbol of the suffocating bell jar painfully obvious. Heckleena says it's Darwinian when Esther's thinking about suicide, but Hairy posts to Facebook that she's just paralyzed by indecision and I can actually relate to that.

As I'm tweeting and updating and blogging, friends and followers are commenting. Someone even adds the hashtag #thebelljar, which means people can track the topic. Really smart people begin to tweet in. I didn't mean to crowd-source this essay, but can I use their ideas? I take the bold step of doing something I have never done. I quote them and give them credit.

Back in the novel Esther has sex with an older dude, and Frannie is shocked and appalled—so am I! No, Mom! Don't do it! The whole thing is frigging exciting, and I'm biting my nails as she's draining a bottle of pills and hiding beneath the house … saved in the nick of time. This woman isn't just trapped in her head, but trapped in her home and a psych ward.

In the end it's not her that commits suicide, but her friend Joan. I'm not sure what to think about the ending. She's not dead. And she seems to be getting better with the cajillion volts of electricity they keep pumping through her.

After copying all the posts, tweets, and blogs, I put it all together in some semblance of an essay format and realize—with a warm feeling in my stomach—that I'm done. I read it over and rewrite bits to make it halfway professional and title it "The Bell Jar: A Discussion Between Friends and Followers."

"Well, holy hullabaloo," I say and then thank all of the people who made it possible. Even Shadownet. I take a picture of my Twitter feed and email it to the principal: *Beautiful*. He may not understand it, but this was one of the most beautiful things that has ever happened to me.

I send the essay to the printer and look up. I'm reflected in the dark plate glass. Black hair shimmers in the computer light, my eyes shining and pink lips puckered like my mom says happens when I'm deep in thought. It's nearly twelve o'clock. With the fresh pages of the essay in my hand, I've done the easy part. I've sixteen hours to restore my life and save my mom's business. Or I'll be as trapped as Esther ever was.

CHAPTER 17

01100100011000010111001001101011011100110110110011010010110
11100110011101100101011100100001011100110111001100101011110100

RISE AND SHINE WORLD! FRANNIE tweets.

Today is gonna be a good good day, Paradise57 posts to his Facebook wall.

I start a Heckleena tweet and then delete it.

Today is all about timing and I have a ton to do. I start packing my bag for the "library."

"I want you to take my shift this morning," my mom says.

I go cold, one hand adding a token textbook to my bag. I can't waste valuable time, but I also can't say no to my mom.

"I read your essay," she continues, "and I think it is brilliant." She's really smiling.

I bite my lip, telling myself that I'm not going to cry. Her belief in me is so unfounded.

"Can I take your shift tomorrow instead?" I ask quietly, wringing my hands.

She squints and I can tell I'm raising her suspicions.

"It's okay," I add. "It's not like I've got anything else to do."

I force a little laugh and she nods.

When I get downstairs, I listen for the sound of the elevator and then rush into the office. I pick up the phone and dial.

"Fenwick?" I say. He sounds really surprised. "I need a mega favor."

I explain and he agrees to come in early to man the cash—but to be really quiet and that I'll pay him for the extra hours myself, not my mom. I'm planning a surprise for her, I tell him. I think the tone for desperate secrecy is the same in any language, and he stops asking questions and finally agrees to help. I gasp with gratitude.

When I take the morning shift, my mom usually stays upstairs until after lunch, so with any luck she'll never know. I'll check on her at ten when Fenwick arrives and will text her at noon that Fenwick is on duty. I really have no idea where I'll be at noon—except that I'll be on my bike huffing. I feel terrible about throwing my mom's trust back in her face but have no choice. The next phase of my plan will begin when Fenwick steps through the door. Until then, I have two hours to twiddle my thumbs.

If I listen hard enough, I can hear the door jangle from downstairs, so I head down to Shadownet. I still haven't reformatted the drives and installed the operating systems, and I wonder whether I'll ever bother. Besides my dad's data, most of what I lost was used to create their Web presences. Until of course all the profiles got hacked. From out of my pack I draw Peter's hard drive.

A hard drive is a small hunk of metal with a whole lot going on inside. I love the heft of it. I flip the hard drive over and over again in my hands. Finally I tap it against the external drive dock, trying to decide whether I should take a peek.

I shake my head clear and type a question into Gumps's green screen.

8-ball question: Should I look in this hard drive?

Answer: *Curiosity killed the cat.*

Huh. Gumps is appearing rather lucid today.

8-ball question: Who is doing this to me?

Answer: *It's best to go last in Russian Roulette.*

I suppose it is, but it doesn't answer my question. I try again.

8-ball question: If you were me, what would you do?

Answer: *Keep your friends close and your enemies closer.*

Three questions, three ominous answers. I try one more, hoping for something optimistic.

8-ball question: Why did the chicken cross the road?

Answer: *Be the change you want to see in the world.* Gumps and Gandhi were close.

I go on my email and let out a shout of glee. The App Store has approved my app. I immediately download it from the store, but while I'm using my phone, I see I have over two thousand notifications. I receive a lot of notifications because of the Facebook and Twitter accounts and stuff, but not like this. These are all texts.

Cold trickles down my back as I open one.

lolololololololololololololololol ... repeated hundreds of times.

The problem with texts is that they cost money. My best guess is someone has cost me over three hundred dollars in the last hour. Another three texts come in while I watch.

I race up to the office and call the phone company. It costs another eight dollars in text messages while I'm on hold, but I manage to get my subscription canceled at least until I sort out what's happening. This really sucks. My iPhone was a big part of my plan today, and now I can use it only if I can access a WiFi network.

"Hello. Miss Janus?" a voice says in a hush.

I jog out of the office. It's Fenwick. I want to hug him for being early and settle for shaking his hand like a jackhammer.

"I work," he says and places a finger to his lips. "You finish surprise, like birthday?"

"Yes, like birthday, only better," I say.

He steps behind the cash and faces the door, probably trying to think of another way to help the business. He's the child my mom should have had.

I move back into the office and shut the door. Time to enact step one of the plan. I take the slip of paper from my pocket with Foxy Lady's license plate and dial the phone number of the police anonymous tip line. What I'm about to do is wrong. I don't know if it's a felony like reading mailing addresses, but I'm positive that I could get into big trouble.

I lower my voice until it's gruff and manly. "Please tell Constable Williams that a woman who is dealing in child pornography on the Web has a black Honda Civic with the license plate Alpha, Juliet, Kilo, X-ray, five, five, five." I pause, uncertain that this will get the reaction I need. "I think I heard screams from the trunk."

I hang up.

"Okay, now I'm in big trouble," I say and run to my bike.

Fenwick waves and makes like he's being really quiet. It would be funny, except I just lied to the police.

I slap my forehead and sprint up to the apartment.

I land before my mom, who is reading.

"Hi ya, Mom, just seeing how you're doing, okay, I think I hear a customer! See you later, love you."

My mom sighs.

"I'm fine," she says. "Don't forget to send your essay in."

"Okay, sure will do, thanks." I sprint out, wondering if I did more damage than good.

It's just after ten and Fenwick will end his shift at four this afternoon, which is when I normally return from school. It's also Jonny's deadline.

The police precinct is a mile away. I pedal hard. I can't imagine the police ignoring my tip and hope I arrive there in time. I also know what I'm doing has moved from stupid to officially dangerous. I'm tracking my enemies. Alone. On a bike.

Which reminds me—I swing to the nearest coffee shop with free WiFi and start the app I made for Jonny.

It's called Canvas, and it's a way of spray painting the world. With the app I can spray paint the side of a building, and anyone with the app can come along and see what I wrote. After I get the app up, I use the tip of my finger to pick pink from a palette of colors and then write in bright letters, *Jan was here first*. And then tap *Publish*. Jonny can use the whole world as his canvas! Isn't that cool? Not that Jonny will ever care now.

I start pedaling again, promising myself to stop at the next closest Starbucks, which I know has WiFi, to mark my trail. Five minutes later I'm in front of the Ottawa Police Precinct. The car pool is in the back, and I ride around, waiting across the street from the huge chain link fence. With any luck, Williams has already been handed the tip and is heading down to her cruiser. I sit for fifteen minutes. Two male cops leave in a big SUV. Another rides a motorcycle, and three depart on bicycles. I'm beginning to wonder if I should have tailed one of the others when Williams tromps out to her vehicle and pulls out.

Here is where my plan starts to breakdown. I'm on a bike. She's in a car. I'm an out-of-shape teenager. Her cruiser has three-hundred horsepower. To keep up, I'm dependent on Ottawa's ridiculously timed lights, guaranteed to snarl traffic. She heads across town. Good news in terms of lights. Lots of them.

I actually stay ahead of her, crossing against traffic, anticipating where she's headed by a block. This works well for about five minutes, until I get stuck unable to cross the busy intersection of Bronson Avenue.

She's still not signaling, though, and drives another block, now ahead of me. I wobble back and forth on the bike as my thighs ache. My socks are already up around my pant cuffs. She turns, and I turn a block early, crossing the street on an angle and earning half a dozen honks. I flip them off. When I reach the next street, she's gone, and I take too many short breaths and feel light-headed. Then I spot it. The cruiser sits beneath a big tree on a rundown street. I bike closer.

Williams stands in a doorway, talking to an unshaven man with a gut and dirty white shirt. Not my target, unless Foxy lives with this guy, but I can't see it. Foxy was halfway to pretty and dressed to the nines. I bring out my iPhone and find another unsecured WiFi network. I paint on the road. *Jan was here next.*

I hide behind a tree while the officer walks to the cruiser. It rumbles to life, does a three-point turn, and starts heading back the way we came. I roll my eyes and turn away so she doesn't see my face as she passes. This was a dead end, some other thing she must have had to check up on. *Come on, Williams!* I said that screams were coming from the trunk of the car.

I wait until Williams pulls into traffic before working to catch up. She turns again and now I manage to cross a street at a light and take the lead. I have it for about six minutes, passing a Starbucks and painting an arrow on the sidewalk as I ease off. Behind me, the cruiser turns. I run into an old woman, nearly knocking her over and sending me over my handlebars. I am too out of breath to apologize, and instead stumble back and forth while gasping. She gives me a crazed look and mutters something in Italian that sounds like a curse. I lurch back on to my bike and cycle around the corner.

Officer Williams threads slowly through a neighborhood that grows seedier with every block. Soon homes have plywood over the windows. One has aluminum foil covering every pane of glass and possible entry, like the real risk isn't gangsters, but rather alien mind-control rays. Police tape crosses the door of another. Weeds overgrow half the yards, paint peels from brick, and chimneys lean with exhaustion.

Finally, Williams hops out of her car. She doesn't have any backup, and I wonder if they take tips like mine seriously enough. I try to guess what house she's targeting and hang back, careful to keep out of the line of site of anyone who might be looking out of a window.

She knocks on the door, then bangs.

Nothing. I run behind a car. Then I dash to the rear of a dumpster across from the house. With my bike hidden, I clamber up the side and risk a look.

There's movement in a window, but no one coming to the door. I get the willies and shiver, squatting down again.

I feel eyes on me, but the house I face is being gutted and there's no glass in the windows. I hear footsteps and curl around the edge of the dumpster. Williams turns around, peers right at me, and then glances left and right. She starts moving, fast. I shrink back, my butt pressing against cold metal. But she's not headed toward me, rather to a car parked on the street several doors away: a black Honda Civic. She knocks on the car trunk and crouches as if listening.

I have my address. My plan is working. I search for an unsecured network, but there's nothing available. The area's dead.

In a few minutes, the constable climbs back into her cruiser and pulls away. I'm alone again, but Williams has done her job. Now it's up to me to figure out the rest.

CHAPTER 18

0110010001100001011100100110101101110011011011011000110100101100
1110011001110110010101110010000101110011011100110010101110100

As I LEAN AGAINST THE cold metal of the dumpster, the time on my screen flips to twelve o'clock. I bite down on my fingers. I have to update my mom, but I have no service. Checking left and then right, it's clear that a Starbucks isn't around the corner in this neighborhood. I need to *warwalk*, which is to search for an unsecure network to rip off. I think it's named after some old movie.

I hop on my bike and sprint across the lawn as quick as I can, hoping that the woman is no longer watching. Several doors down, I relax and hold my phone with one hand, cycling slowly along the street until I find an open connection.

A network pops up on my phone and asks if I want to connect—it's a good signal too. I agree and boot up the Canvas app. I write the address of Foxy Lady's house all over the street in neon green. Satisfied that I've marked my trail, but feeling a little like Gretel before she steps into the witch's house, I send my mom an email—I'm doing well, getting lots done, Fenwick's at the store, etc. It's vague enough not to be lying, I figure. I also prepare an email to Jonny.

Dearest Jonny, I'm such an idiot and you're so cool and I know I AM a freak and ...

I delete it all and try again:

Jonny, I'm totally sorry about yesterday and everything else. I made something for you. Happy Painting. I include a link to the Canvas app in the App Store.

Another email.

Hey Karl, sorry I've been acting so weird. Hopefully I can explain later.

And then that's all there is to do. I feel like I've just said my goodbyes. But I'd be crazy to break into the house with the car parked outside. What if she's home? I'm sure someone moved in the upstairs window. I have to wait. If nothing happens by two o'clock, I'll rethink my plan.

To stake out the place, I first need to hide. A woman takes laundry in while a baby crawls at her feet. On the horizon, clouds bruised deep purple are chewing through what's left of the blue sky. I can't just sit on the curb, and if I huddle beside the dumpster all day, someone is liable to call the cops on me.

I bike slowly back down the street toward Foxy's house. I could hide in the house being renovated, but my gut tells me that the best spot is inside the dumpster itself. Being across from my target, the dumpster's perfect, offering a good view of the house if I peer over the edge. I lean the bike against the rear of it and climb inside to duck down, breathless and listening for sounds of my discovery.

I hear nothing. But the blackening sky weighs on my forehead with the combined force of a billion raindrops.

Do I have a plan as I squat amidst the six garbage bags that someone tossed in? The bags have split, spilling out old milk cartons, coffee grinds, and banana peels. All recyclable and compostable, I note, and reeking. My plan is to stay until I hear a car leave and then see if it was her car. That's it. Once she's gone, I break in.

I settle down to wait, slipping a clean piece of drywall between me and the garbage. I may not be able to use my phone for much right now, but there's nothing like some Angry Birds to pass the time. I play for what seems like an hour, but is only fifteen minutes, and am startled by the sound of footsteps. Stealthy footsteps and whispers. Someone knows I'm here ... I need to hide.

I look at the garbage and my stomach curdles like the oozing milk. The hushed voices are nearing. Careful not to scuff the metal bottom or sides of the dumpster, I lie down beside the bags and roll one over my feet. I gag and draw the next across my legs. Something wet trickles over my jeans. I cover my chest, and the final bag I pick up and hold just shy of my face. It's heavy and I turn away so that the cold, slimy plastic presses against the side of my head. The bag muffles the whispers. I try not even to breathe.

Something scratches along the metal. I realize that the sound is coming from inside the bin: claws. I whimper. A rat trundles past, stops, pauses to look me over with pink, beady eyes, and then continues down to my toes and the mess of peels and coffee grinds.

Suddenly, the side of the dumpster rings with a gong. I cry out. Whoever they are run away, yelling. I wait for another minute until their shouts are echoes and then ease the garbage off.

Orange juice, rotten vegetables, and fruit slime, along with other, less identifiable scabs of old food, are oiling my jeans and shirt. I dry heave before regaining control of my stomach. The rat is nowhere to be seen, but its memory sends shudders down my spine. I get to my knees and slowly stand to peer over the edge. One black Honda Civic is still parked. But something's missing: my bike.

I drop back down and lean against the side of the bin. I could make it back home by four if I left right now. Does sixty minutes of biking make two hours of walking? Maybe more, I guess. And I'm tired. I need to make a decision.

I don't have the proof I need, only the address of some woman who dropped off a computer. It occurs to me that I still don't know how she wound up with the computer. Did Jonny sell it? Was it stolen? Not that it matters. Jonny's going to go to the cops regardless. I look at my jeans. There's no way my mom will believe I was at the library, not smelling like a landfill. I'll email her when I've solved the mystery, or I'll take a cab. Until then, I'm on stake out.

Another hour passes, and with it several cars, two door slams, another round of kids—one of whom spits a wad of gum on to me—and it's starting to rain.

The rain reminds me of crying and crying reminds me of Jonny. The warm press of him when he was wet. The heat of his lips. His artistry and his hands. I search through my camera roll and pull up the pictures from under the bridge. I smile and wish I'd taken a photo of his painting with all the flowers. He's probably covered over them both since. I feel a pang of loss and clench my eyes shut.

I smile at the image of him I have in my head and then realize I'm confused because Jonny is looking a little more like Karl with every passing second and it's his lips and hands I feel and this time I let them wander.

The sky breaks open and it starts to pour, flushing the heat of my thoughts away. My clothes are soaked but at least they're cleaner. The cold shower brings me back to the fact that I need to make another choice. Jonny may have already made the choice for me, but that doesn't mean I can stop thinking about him. Both Karl and Jonny fulfill parts of me. Jonny's a bit of a loner though, and I don't need more loneliness in my life. He's also artistic and sensitive. Karl, on the other hand, is really social and appreciates the tech-me. I can see myself teaching him how to make apps too.

A car starts and peels out on the wet pavement. Hoping beyond hope, I hold my iPhone over the edge and take a picture of the street. Looking at the image I see a gaping hole where the Civic had been. The street has pulled its rotten tooth, and the rain suddenly seems like a boon. No one will be out to see me. It's time for me to take action, but now that it's really happening, I'm paralyzed.

I've been here before. When my mom first got sick, and Dad left, I almost gave up. My mom couldn't run the store. She could barely make it to the washroom. I could have called in the authorities and we would have shut down the business. If I had, I don't know where we'd be now or how my mom would feel. I'll never know. I didn't give up then. I put my head down and learned what I needed to learn to keep the business afloat. I nursed my mom. I finished my homework, and I created Shadownet to keep me company. I struggled. I am not going to waste all of that effort.

I clamber over the side of the dumpster and dash across the road. It's raining so hard that the drops are striking the puddles and bouncing back a foot. I'm sopping. My fist slams against the door to the house. It's better to figure out now if anyone remains home. A thrill runs through me as I realize I'm about to break and enter. That's another felony today. Karl was right. Maybe I am a bad girl, a Black Hat Hacker. Maybe Karl and I are more alike than Jonny and I could ever be.

There's no answer to my banging. No one home, or at least no one answering.

I try the handle. Locked.

Am I taking this too far? The sheeting rain needles my head with cold heavy drops. I look back to the empty road and then to the house. With a sharp nod, I hurdle the short porch railing and sidle through the windowless alleyway between the houses. The eaves keep the rain off and it feels like I'm exploring a cave until I break into the backyard. It's little bigger than a postage stamp of weeds, enclosed in a green chain-link fence.

A small porch overhangs the yard from the second floor. The second-story porch door might be open, but I'm not a great climber. I test the two window wells into the basement and then the sliding door on the ground floor. They're all locked.

I contemplate the cave-like alley. It's now or never. No one knows I'm here, so no one will know it was me. Other yards surround this one, but they are all dark and veiled by the driving rain. Rain like this doesn't last long, and for now it's loud.

I search the weeds and my fingers close about a fist-sized rock. Hefting it once, I take three steps back and launch the stone at the sheet of plate glass. I miss. It hits the brick and rolls back down the steps.

I try again, and this time the sliding door breaks into a million cracks and the rock leaves a small hole where it struck. I gulp and listen for evidence that someone heard, or a house alarm. But there's only rain.

I jog to the door and kick more of the glass inside. It's all stuck together on a film and it takes a full minute of kicking before I have a hole large enough to duck through. Inside, the walls feel close until my eyes adjust. The only light is the dull gray of the storm through the other side of the sliding door. My shoes crunch over broken glass. My chest hurts. My head aches and I want to vomit like my Frannie Mouthwater doll.

I have entered the lair of my worst enemy.

CHAPTER 19

011001000110000101110010011010110111001101101100011010010110
1110011001110110010101110010000101110011011100110010101110100

THE SMELL HITS ME FIRST. A sweet fragrance fills the air as if tendrils of the woman's perfume have formed a sticky web. My stomach churns. Outside, thunder rumbles across the sky.

Once I had to check on the Shadownet server in the middle of a thunderstorm. I crept down the basement steps, the rain rattling off the roof high above and wind moaning through whatever crevice it could find. My having spent half my life on the Internet seemed to make real-world weather and noises even scarier. Every shadow menaced. Every cranny held a black and sinister creature. Every sound was the whisk of a knife. I never made it to the bottom of the steps. I knocked the flashlight against the stair railing and it went out. I ran back upstairs screaming so my mom would know when they caught me. Would know to get out.

I'm a total wimp.

As I move deeper into the house, rain hammers the roof in

waves. Glass is scattered over a brown linoleum floor. The rock I threw has shattered a pitcher of milk, drenching a newspaper and the table it resided on. An island with a stove looks out on the disaster area, but there is nothing for me here except to learn that she drinks skim milk, reads *The Sun*, and sucks at crosswords. I start to shiver from my soaked clothing and leave puddles with every step.

Once out of the kitchen I stand in a bare hallway. To my right and left are doors. I peek inside the one on my right. It leads to the basement. Steps disappear into darkness. No chance I'm going down there. When I open the left-hand door, I fall back and slam into the wall. Beady marble eyes stare back at me, and it takes a moment for me to recognize the dead foxes. I toe the closet door shut and draw a shuddering breath.

The closet is beneath the stairway leading up from the front door. Near the entry is an opening into a living area. Floorboards creak with every step I take. A red corduroy couch occupies half the room, its ribbing so worn it's pink where you'd sit. Beside the couch looms a lamp, out of kilter from its base. The only things decorating scuffed burgundy walls are the unlikely poster of the band Clash and another of Chris Isaak. The only song I know from Chris Isaak cycles through my skull: *Baby did a bad, bad thing.* A lounge chair and an IKEA shelf chock full of books complete the rather transient and masculine feel.

I look back toward the basement and then up the stairs. Maybe the woman went for groceries and she's already on her way back. I have to hurry. I need an office. An office will have a computer and a computer will have evidence.

The first step groans, and I swallow the lump in my throat. Without lights, the dreariness shrouds me like a cold blanket. My teeth chatter uncontrollably. At the top, I pause with my hand on the light switch. I'm eager to dispel the shadows, but light would be visible from anyone watching, or coming home.

At the hall closet, I open the doors to find a mismatched set of sheets and a bag of toilet paper.

Besides the closet, two bedrooms and a bathroom are on the upper level. One is filled with boxes. I check their sides and find they're mostly from wine stores, but one of them has Cyrillic writing on it. Russian, Ukrainian, Czech? I can't know, but it makes me think about the Russian Frannie skyped, the one with the shark eyes. Not for the first time today, I realize I'm in over my head.

I skip the bathroom and head into the master. The covers of a barren double bed are tangled. A side table has a box of tissue paper and a novel, again in Cyrillic. Twin doors lead out onto the porch I'd seen from the yard. In the corner are two black iron balls and a small desk with a laptop computer whose screen saver repeats a psychedelic design. Bingo. But before I head to the computer, I stop and stare.

Several medals hang on the walls, a few indecipherable university degrees, and two photos. My fingers slide down the side of a picture frame, forcing it crooked. It's a photo of Foxy, and she's beautiful. She has noble features and carefully applied, but dramatic makeup. Today she's a shadow of her former self. It's the second photo that restarts my teeth chattering. I draw back a step and clench my hands into fists.

In the frame, a man lifts twin iron balls above his head, holding on to black grips with meaty fists. His arms are thick with muscle, tendons arrow up his neck, and his legs bulge. Even with the Cyrillic below I know what I'm seeing. This is Fenwick, National Kettlebell Champion.

A door slams.

For a moment I wonder if it was the neighbor's. Then I hear a voice. I run to the porch door and throw it open. The height hits me with a wave of vertigo and my vision tunnels. I turn back inside; my heart is wedged in my esophagus. My options are to leap off the railing or to risk the stairs and confrontation. The computer screen whirls.

I race to it and tap the keyboard to bring up a browser. A woman yells in what I guess to be Russian or Estonian. No one speaks back to her, so she's either crazy or on her phone, probably with Fenwick. In ten seconds I have Heckleena's Twitter account up. I could have emailed my mom, but she's crippled, or Jonny, but he hates me. Besides, neither checks their email regularly. Given how many crimes I've committed, telling anyone who would go to the police doesn't seem like a good idea. I suppose I'm not really thinking straight. So for better or for worse, I tweet this:

Help me! Use Canvas app.

In the hall below, the language grows harsh with anger; she's returning from the kitchen. The only weapon are the two kettlebells. I grip the handles on one and strain, lifting it slowly to my knee. It's too heavy. I go to set it down, but drop it. The kettlebell slams into floor. The steps creak and creak.

I could hide in the closet or under the bed, but then I'd be entirely trapped and who wouldn't look there? I flip the laptop closed and pause. On the back of the lid is a giant happy face. The laptop from the medical clinic! All roads lead to Fenwick.

I jump back on the porch and shut the door. Rain sluices over me. The doors have big windows, but if I climb over the side of the railing, someone might miss me. I swing my foot up and over and hang in mid air with my feet braced on the bottom, hands holding the spindles. The rain continues to fall. As I hang it occurs to me that I've left a trail of wet right outside to my hiding place.

If I drop, I'll break my spine on the fence. Could I have fashioned a rope from the sheets and swung down? Perhaps in my next life I'll be smart.

I hear a sound. But it's not the door opening. It's a click, like the sound of a lock snapping home. Why would she lock the door? I debate climbing back up, but it's no good now, not if the door is locked. I'd have to break in, which she'd hear and she'd catch me. Suddenly I understand what has happened. The only escape I have is down. She eliminated one escape route and left me with just one choice.

And there she is. Ten feet beneath me, my last exit gone. She's smirking, but her eyes are cold and professional, those of a killer.

So I jump. And for a second I have the satisfaction of wiping that smile right off of her face. I could see myself as trapped, but instead I prefer to see her as a mattress. I push away from the porch with a sharp cry and twist midair. I watch her eyes widen as I fall. I'm sure my eyes are like saucers until I clench them shut for impact.

But Foxy isn't a mattress. She's bony and the bones stick out at angles, and her muscles are ribbons of steel. Only her lungs have any give and they collapse as I land on them with my knees, ankle twisting beneath with a sickening snap. Pain races up my leg. I roll over her, get up, the adrenaline covering the worst of my injury. I don't dare look back. I'm at the fence when a hand grabs my collar. My ankle feels aglow. The shirt tears, but something hard presses into my kidney.

It's chill. A gun.

That someone has a gun pressed into my side is difficult to grasp. It's surreal. I break into someone's home, discover my mom's employee wants me out of the way for some reason I can't fathom, and now his partner in crime jabs a gun barrel in me?

It's a lot to take in. I might have kept going too, and maybe she wouldn't have shot me, but my ankle catches on the fence top and I see something very wrong.

My ankle is bent so that with my leg up, instead of the toe pointing out to the left where it should, it points down where it shouldn't. As if seeing it makes it real, pain surges into my stomach and I begin to vomit.

Dark corners crowd out the light and my vision blurs. I wobble, catch my already broken ankle on the fence, and collapse.

CHAPTER 20

0110010001100001011100100110101101110011011011000110100101 10
11100110011101100101011100100010110011011100110010101110100

PAIN SHOOTS THROUGH MY LEG, and with each throb of my heart, pulses of agony surge to my brain. I've never broken anything before; the torture is paralyzing. If I move, I'll black out. I can't see a thing, but at least I'm conscious, shaking with cold, but alive.

A thick paste fills my mouth. I might have been out for hours. My head feels woolly and I try to remember everything that has happened. The only thing seared into the hard drive of my mind is the image of my foot, dangling. My stomach heaves, but produces nothing. Just then I realize that it's not dark; my eyes are clenched against the pounding in my ankle.

I open my eyes.

I'm in the basement. The two windows to the backyard filter gray light through their grime. A furnace clicks on and roars to life, the gas flames flickering blue like tiny demons dancing in a ring. I listen for voices or footsteps but hear none. Another hum rises above the furnace. It's familiar. I'd know it anywhere. It's the purr of computer servers.

My arms stretch behind my neck, the hands tied to a metal desk. My foot thumps with anguish. I'm still wearing my shoes, and it's causing part of the problem by constricting blood flow. With the toe of my good sneaker I touch the heel of my bad foot. I cry out and bite my lip from the pain. It's too late to take the shoe off. I can only hope the shoe won't cut off blood flow and make it a gangrenous foot. But I have bigger things to worry about. Survival.

I don't wear a watch and my iPhone is nowhere to be seen, so I can't tell how late it is. My mom might not even know I'm missing yet, and as for Heckleena's tweet? I don't watch my own feed, so how can I expect anyone else to? Not to mention that tweets disappear in about a minute off most people's feeds and anyone who did catch it probably thought it was a joke or lives a million miles away. If no one has saved me yet, they're not coming. I'd even take the police. The only others who know I'm here are Foxy and Fenwick—Fenwick, who could be holding my mom hostage too.

I have to help her.

I roll to my right so that I can see the area nearest the front of the house. More boxes are piled there, most of them unopened. A ladder leans against a concrete wall with several large bottles of cleaning solvents and paint cans. The water heater is tucked under the stairs, which descend into the middle of the single room. It looks like a regular basement. On the wall opposite me I see the alarm system—which is evidently a silent alarm and likely what brought Foxy home early. It's all the stuff on the far right that's out of place. Alien to any normal home, definitely weird for this neighborhood, and just about the last thing I'd expect to see here: a rack of servers.

Not just any rack, this is one of those professional jobs. If you've ever seen a baker's cooling rack for cookie sheets then you have a sense of what it looks like. This one is black and has sixteen slots for servers. All sixteen of them are filled with blinking green lights. A twist of blue wires descends from it and runs up to the ceiling, where it disappears. Beside the servers are an eclectic group of computer towers, all piled one atop the other in a grid of beige, black and white. At least fifty, all humming, all connected to the professional rack. Evidently, the sixteen servers weren't providing enough juice and he needed to supplement them with the older boxes.

What would Fenwick use servers for? The guy is good with his hands but I never thought he understood computers. I'm looking at over a hundred grand in technology.

The servers scare me as much as the gun had. Both point to a more professional operation, and if I add in the acting of Foxy and the infiltration of Fenwick into Assured Destruction, then I have to assume these guys are doing this for good reason, an investment they'd do anything to protect. The edges of my vision grow dark again and I fight off unconsciousness by taking deep slow breaths. If I'm going to escape, I have to stay lucid. I need a way to signal the cops, or to break free and reach help. At this point I don't even care about Assured Destruction, or my expulsion. I just want to see my mom.

I half-heartedly twist around, but no, my teeth can't reach the bindings. Surprise. I inspect my wrists. Tight to the flesh are two translucent plastic ties. I don't know if they're the kind cops use, but I can't budge them and it cuts into my skin to try. The ties are threaded through a hole in the metal drawer of the desk and the edges are not sharp enough to cut the plastic. I strain against the ties; the increase in blood pressure causes my ankle to ache in rebellion. The desk moves an inch and I slump back to the floor. But as I lie on the cold concrete, my heart thuds in my chest. I'm grinning ... the desk moved a whole inch.

I look around again with a keener eye. I inspect the furnace. Gas lines must feed it. I could break the lines, cause a leak and let the entire house explode?

My mouth tightens. Perhaps not so great an idea if one of my criteria is staying alive. The ladder is useless. The paint and cleaning solvents—maybe not. The boxes? Other than the servers, there's little else that could be useful. I have to try something before dark descends and my only light will be from the twinkling of data flowing over Fenwick's lines.

I don't want an explosion, but I do want smoke. A part of me likes the concept of revenge. I know how expensive servers are. I also know how much time it takes to set everything up and, of course, then there's the content residing on the servers. It's all valuable or it wouldn't be there. Poetic justice, Principal Wolzowski called it—when the punishment matches the crime.

I haul on the desk and gain another inch. The desk legs screech against the concrete. I hold my breath. No activity upstairs that I can hear. I decide it's better to make a lot of noise quickly, rather than drag it out.

I'm sitting up, looking down at my swollen foot and calf. My head is between my arms, which are stretched back and on an angle. Each time I throw my weight forward against my arms, the desk moves. A little. Between pulls I don't bother to listen for sounds of people coming. Instead, I lunge forward, grimace against the pain, and lunge forward again. One, two, three … Ugh! One, two, three … Ugh! I haul.

My arms feel as though they're ripping from their sockets. Inch by inch, I reach the paint. The broken ankle sends tears to my eyes with each movement. Slick blood coats my wrists where the ties rub my skin raw. I take a few deep breaths to calm myself and to blink away tears.

With my good foot, I turn each of the labels of the containers, looking for the campfire symbol for flammable. I'm in luck. A can of paint, three quarters full. Its lid is even open a crack. My plan might just work. I shove the can with my foot toward the servers and move it several feet. Then I drag the desk closer. Shove the paint. Drag desk. Shove paint. Desk. Paint.

Fresh pain lances through my leg and down into my shoulders from my wrists. I grit my teeth and shove the paint further. Desk. Paint. Desk-paint.

Finally I'm at the servers with my can of flammable paint.

Now for the tricky part. I lodge the can of paint between my calves and haul upward. I manage to lift it only a few servers high. I'm not sure if that's high enough for what I want, but my first task is to snap the lid off. Holding the can between my calves, I bang it hard against the servers, trying to catch the lip of the lid on a bracket. When I do so, the agony nearly renders me unconscious. The can slips and crashes to the floor. The smell of paint blankets me. Its stringent odor brings me back. It stinks like something that can burn.

Liquid seeps out of the can, beginning to form a pool. I panic, madly collecting the can between my thighs and turning it right side up. My jeans are coated in the same burnt red coating the living-room walls upstairs. But I have half an open can of paint. A skin had formed on top from it being left open, but there is plenty of liquid paint still left.

I wriggle until the can sits between my calves and then, with all my might, I swing my legs up and with them the can. I'm jackknifed and shaking from the effort of holding the position. The blood draining from my ankle hurts more than ever. My vision begins to tunnel from the suffering. I twist my legs and lean to the servers. Paint begins to drizzle out of the sideways can. I twist more. More paint. It's syrupy and drips on the servers' sides.

I begin to jerk from the exertion; the paint glugs a little farther out, rather than just drooling down the face of the servers. I jerk the can on purpose. A chug slops over the servers, seeping through the ventilation grills in the gear. Heaving the can back and forth, I douse the equipment as far back as the paint will go. My muscles spasm and my legs drop to the third server down, then the second. First. With a final haul of my legs, the can hits the floor and rolls. My feet slump and pain screams up my leg. I faint.

I wake to smoke.

Smoke hugs the ceiling, pooling in great oily billows. It's what I wanted. Perhaps more than I wanted. It's dark. I can't tell if that's because the smoke is blocking the light from the windows, or if it's night. Flickering orange sparks highlight the smoke like a miniature thunderstorm; next to me, the servers sizzle and twitch with death throes of their own.

A small lick of flame spurts from a vent in one of the boxes. The fire slips down the side, following the trail of paint, spreading fast. This wasn't in the plan.

I look down at the red covering me. My mind slowly rolls through the implications. The paint looks an awful lot like blood.

CHAPTER 21

0110010001100001011100100110101101110011011011011000110100101 10
1110011001110110010101110010000101110011011100110010101110100

F IRE TRACKS DOWN THE PAINT like a lit fuse. I'm stiff from my time unconscious and my legs don't respond right away. The flames suddenly accelerate and reach the side of my pants, but instead of turning my legs into torches, the flame stops, unable to make the leap to the cotton. Suddenly I realize, I'm still soaking wet and the rain has saved me.

My jeans begin to steam and I wince from the heat of the fire. My eyes burn with fumes. Inch by inch, I shift my legs out of the puddle of paint. The fire soon reduces it to a black patch of tar on the concrete. Finally the flames on the floor extinguishes. The third server up from the floor burns steadily, however, flames licking over the edge of the fourth. It's only a matter of time before the whole stack is ablaze.

I throw my weight against the desk and it shifts a half an inch from the fire. But then I stop to think about what I am doing. The smoke bumping up against the ceiling has lowered a foot; if I don't get out of here, the smoke will choke me. That's the more immediate threat. I can't depend on enough smoke escaping to alert a neighbor.

I look around. There's no way to cut my binds. I'm not strong enough to haul the desk up the stairs, so what can I do? If I stay, I burn or asphyxiate. I stare at the flames and they're hypnotic. The same way ocean waves lap at a shore, tongues of fire lap at the servers' edges. The fire's color changes to green as it pick up flecks of copper, or even red and blue as other precious metals imbedded in the server's circuitry cook. A flare of white brings me back. I have an idea. It's a little crazy.

It may have been six years since we covered conduction in science class but it's amazing what comes back to you when you need it.

The desk moves an inch. But this time, instead of moving away, it shifts toward the fire. I pull again. Another inch.

I cough as a swirl of smoke dips down and into my lungs.

I yank again. I heave. Finally, with my legs covered in the burnt charcoal of the paint residue, the desk nudges against the server rack. Flames run from the servers to curl beneath the underside of the metal desk. I tuck my head, slippery with sweat, between my arms to escape the baking flames. I feel like a rotisserie chicken. The heat is growing, the ceiling lowering.

Upstairs I hear nothing. No shouts of alarm, no footsteps. No one is coming.

My arm closest to the fire blisters. Tears stream from my eyes and dry just as fast. Every so often I rest the back of my hand against the metal of the drawer to which I'm strapped. It's burning hot—maybe that will be enough.

I rub the plastic ties against it. Back and forth. Praying for them to melt. Nothing. The heat through my jeans is frying my leg. I can feel the flesh cooking, but the metal is taking longer to heat and I try to distract myself by recalling the math. Silver is the most conductive metal, then copper, then ... where did steel rank? I test the metal again; it's searing. I jerk the ties back and forth, back and forth, and then haul down on them. They snap and my head cracks against the floor.

I am dazed. I'm free.

Liquid plastic drools on to the floor from the server casings. I roll further away, wincing as my broken ankle swings with me. The only possible exits are the stairs and the windows. I can break the windows, but can I fit through their narrow openings? With my ankle, can I use the ladder to climb up and out?

I decide on the stairs and drag myself. I keep my ankle splinted against my other good ankle and slide across the floor using my arms. It reminds me of how my mom sometimes needs to get around, when her legs have totally given out and she can't make it to her chair. It's slow, painful, and frustrating. I feel for her. I understand her a bit more. I miss her.

I won't let her down. She's all I have. I ignore the new pains in my forearms, but commando crawling is easier than dragging a desk. Finally, with my back to the bottom stair, I place my palms on it and push myself upward until my butt sits on the wooden step. I draw a deep breath. The whole basement dances crazily in the firelight.

I shift my hands to the next stair and press upward. Another step higher, I press up again. I count twenty steps, and by the time I reach halfway, my triceps are aching, my foot is impossibly swollen, and I have to lean forward to keep my head out of the smoke. The servers are now a column of greasy flames. I note that the nearby boxes have also begun to smolder—my time is even shorter than I'd thought. The ceiling, when in view, is black and charred.

I push up onto the next step. The higher I go, the worse the smoke. My lungs rebel and I cough and hack, still pushing higher, aiming for the doorknob that sometimes can be seen within the murk. On the seventeenth step, my eyes sting and my body spasms with racking coughs. My foot hurts so much, and I'm tempted to reach for the doorknob but know it's still too far—impossibly far. I feel light headed and sleepy. I can't tell if it's due to the smoke or because I'm dying, but everything is shadows. I shut my eyes against the irritating fumes and lie back against the stairs.

Suddenly my world brightens, snapping me out of my funk. The boxes have burst into a bonfire, burning like a pile of birch bark. The billows of heat push the smoke away from the staircase, clearing a passage to the door that immediately begins to close. I manage two more steps.

I pause on the nineteenth stair to cough again and slump over the final step onto the landing. The door is to my right. My head is pressed against the cool wood. I watch the smoke slip beneath the door jam. I wait for a series of spasms of coughing to fade and then reach for the doorknob. I twist, lusting after the clean air beyond, for its cool balm.

The doorknob doesn't budge. Locked.

Boxes tumble from the pile, boxes filled with old computer equipment and books—equipment that probably came from Assured Destruction and highly flammable books that probably came from Ellie Wise's house. These now burn against the stairs, blocking the path of anyone wanting to reach the windows. Blocking me.

The solvents explode in a ball of flame, and I shield my face, feeling my hair curl and catching a whiff of its burning.

The fire crackles and roars as it sucks precious oxygen into its hungry throat. I cough again, slumped, weakening as my fist knocks at the door. A cloud envelopes me. I'm going to die. I'm sorry it came to this, and I hate that my mother may never know what happened. Maybe Fenwick will get away with his plans. Maybe Jonny won't even attend my funeral. I won't have a chance to make up with my mom. I curl at the landing, lips sucking for air through the crack beneath the door.

The next bright light I see, I presume to be heaven. But this heaven has a creature waving its arms and choking on the heavenly, swirly haze, which isn't quite white enough to convince me of a celestial origin.

My eyes are filled with tears, so I can't see well, but when the figure bends closer and says something that's muffled by the roar of the fire, I make out the identity of my angel. It's not whom I expect. Not whom I expect at all.

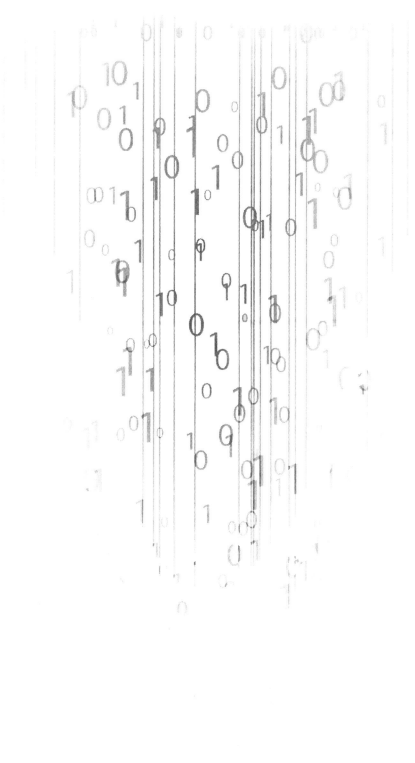

CHAPTER 22

0110010001100001011100100110101101110011011011000110100101 10
11100110011101100101011100100010011100110111001100101011101 00

P ETER.

Good, old Peter stares down at me, his face a mask of concern between intermittent coughs. I reach out to him, and he snatches my arm, dragging me from the stairwell and into the hallway. I scream in pain from his grip around my tender wrists. He kneels when we're several feet into the hall. I fall against his shoulder and draw deep clean breaths of air.

He examines my purple and black ankle.

"We have to get you to a hospital," he says. "What's going on?"

I try to explain but my voice is hoarse. "How'd? How—"

He holds up his iPhone and the map indicating where I'd left my graffiti tags. The guy follows Heckleena on Twitter? I start to laugh, but hack instead. Smoke pours out of the stairwell, and Peter leaves me to slam the basement door shut.

When he closes it, Fenwick stands there.

My eyes still hurt from the smoke and it's hard for me to

speak. Only a rasping bark leaves my throat. Fenwick's mouth twists into a snarl.

Fenwick grabs Peter around the neck with his beefy arm. Peter's eyes fly wide and his hands clutch at his captor. He loses his footing and falls backward into Fenwick.

To my amazement, though, the fall is faked. Peter leaps back and shoves Fenwick into the doorframe between the kitchen and hall. Fenwick's head glances off, and Peter rips free of the grip, delivering an uppercut to Fenwick's gut. He doubles over. Peter brings his fists down on the nape of Fenwick's neck, collapsing him to the floor. Peter breathes hard over top. Not bad for an old dude.

On the ground Fenwick's palms are flat against the carpet in a push-up position. Then he looks at me. And smiles. His legs snap around Peter's, catching them at the knee and twisting. Peter topples with a shout of surprise—he doesn't have a chance.

"Go!" Peter screams. I begin to haul myself toward the front door, ignoring the pain. The smack of fists into flesh come from behind. I draw sharp quick breaths. Black scorches climb the wall of the living room; paint bubbles. This whole place is about to erupt. I enter the cool tile of the foyer, but the door bursts open and standing there is Foxy—with her gun.

As I stare into the barrel, smoke leaves the entry in a plume. It's only a matter of time before the fire department is called, but it takes less time to pull a trigger.

"You're a pain in the ass," the woman says and reaches down to snare my wrist. Funny, but my ass is the one part of me that doesn't hurt. I've got nothing left with which to fight. Foxy kicks the door closed and drags me into the living room. I lie motionless on the shag carpet. It's hot and I imagine I'm just above the licking flames of the servers. I bite my lip when I see the bloodied face of Peter as he's hauled into the living room semi-conscious, eyes fluttering.

"Why, Fenwick?" I ask. "Why are you doing this?"

For the first time I see the true Fenwick. His black eyes burn and his finger points like Foxy's gun.

"Why? I nothing here." He's shaking. I doubt any of this was part of his plan. "Nothing. I do jobs. Lot of jobs. But … no money." He shakes his head. "In Estonia I computer scientist. Here I paint house. I clean house. When I get job with your mother I see what I need. What you have …" He trails off.

"And you want it. You want to be a computer recycler."

He squints and then begins to chuckle. It's an ugly laugh and I want it to stop.

"I no want recycle. I keep like you. Social security numbers, passports, birthdays, hard drives remember everything. Then I make big server farm and let people look at pretty pictures." He relaxes, hooking his thumbs into tight jeans.

I finally see it. He wants to mine the hard drives for identity theft. Worse still, to run a pornography ring. He's started a series of porn sites and wants to grow it using old computers customers bring in to run them.

"But why hurt my friends?"

"You get caught with hard drives, mommy lose business," he smirks. "She like me. I buy."

I don't know why he's smiling in all this. He can't get the business now. She doesn't like him anymore. If he kills us, he'll have to run. Surely they'll know who it was.

He looks over at the wall. The scorch marks climb higher and thicken. I see the posters curling and it occurs to me that I could have figured this all out a lot sooner if I'd been a bit smarter. Chris Isaac has a song where the lyrics go: *Baby did a bad, bad thing.* It's the same language Fenwick used in Frannie's email—and the same song he was singing when I came home a few days ago. If I die here, I want to come back as an elephant so I'll have a better memory. Unfortunately, what I deserve is to come back as a worm and not a very smart one.

Fenwick pulls out a phone and dials.

"I back. Have daughter and boyfriend," he says. "Nice tries."

"Mom!" I shout, realizing to whom he's talking. Realize whom he must have been visiting while I fried his servers.

"Sign papers and give me business and I let them go."

"Don't do it, Mom!"

Foxy strides to me and slaps me across the face. Tears well in my eyes.

"Tell anyone, I find you." His tone menaces. "Sign. Scan. Send to me. If ever you contact police, I be sure to kill your little girl—just try. I have friends."

I swallow the lump in my throat.

"You're going to jail whatever happens. You can't run a porn business out of Assured Destruction," I say.

"Oh, little computer girl? Porn not illegal. Not destroying hard drives illegal. Breaking into house illegal."

Porn is wrong, but I realize I've got nothing. I can't prove he hacked my network and did all those other things; they were designed to call attention to what I was doing, not to benefit him. I only have tapes showing his girlfriend coming into the store. We have a better run operation because of him, and I'd lied to the police. What could I actually prove? Even Peter's first question to me was about what was going on.

"So, little, poor girl? You break into my house to rob me and cause fire. Very bad."

My mom must be saying something back to him in the phone, because he clutches it tighter to his ear.

"Da," he says into the phone, checks his email, and then grins at Foxy, who nods back. "Da."

"Now we save you," he grins at me. "Fenwick is hero."

Fenwick bends and shoulders Peter, whose eyes are still

partially rolled back into his skull. The carpet has begun to melt and Foxy drags me through scalding puddles of it. I cry out and suddenly I'm being lifted in strong arms while Foxy shouts at whomever is holding me, but at least her gun is gone, hidden away. Hidden until it's needed again to enforce whatever my mom has agreed to.

I can hear other shouts and people; I try to look back at my rescuer but it's smoky, my eyes are watering, and the man is hunkered down over top of me so I can't see his face through the tangle of my hair.

We break into dusk. Fire trucks barrel down the block and a crowd of onlookers gather as smoke whirls into an evening colored red by the decaying sun.

"Janus!" someone calls.

I blink my eyes clear and brush away my hair. Ellie stands with the onlookers, and beside her I make out Hannah and Harry. What was everyone doing here?

Standing at the end of the walk is Jonny. His hands are tucked into his pockets and he's gritting his teeth. But if that's Jonny, then who is ...?

I look back at my transportation, catching as I do the warning glare of Foxy at our side. A pair of startlingly blue eyes gaze down at me. My arms are wrapped around the neck of Karl.

"How'd you—?"

"Doesn't everyone follow Heckleena?" His smile rends my heart in two. "We were all wondering who it was. So cool it's you."

When I look back toward Jonny, he's already walking down the street into the flashes of oncoming emergency vehicles. Flames boogie in the living-room window of the house and I suspect nothing inside can be saved. Not the servers, not the evidence, not the happy-face laptop. My actions have cleared the way for Fenwick.

Karl lays me on to a gurney, and a worried paramedic inspects my ankle and another the burns on my arms. Nearby, Peter stares at me, lucid but with a trail of blood running from his hairline.

"Thanks, Peter."

"Nothing to thank me for," he replies and glances to see Fenwick lurking in the shadows.

"Don't say anything, okay?" I ask and he studies my face. "My mom wouldn't want you to say anything right now."

"The police—" he begins.

"I know, but it isn't over," I vow as I'm lifted into the ambulance. Peter gives a little hopeless wave, either a goodbye or a signal of surrender.

CHAPTER 23

01100100011000010111001001101011011100110110110010011010010110
11100110011101100101011100100010110011011100110010101110100

T HE OPERATION ON MY ANKLE takes three hours but is over in a blink—for me at least. In post-op I'm drowsy when they show me an X-ray of my ankle with three pins through it. A cast wraps my foot and climbs up to my knee. When I see the cast, all I can think of is Jonny having a new canvas to doodle upon.

Finally they wheel me out of post-op, and from down the hall, the small squeaks of wheels steadily grow louder. A smile cracks my lips, and my mom shoots beside me, grabs my hand, and buries her face in it.

"Janus," she says. "Janus."

And I'm crying and she's crying. "I'm sorry, Mom." My throat hurts.

"You're okay, you're going to be fine." Her tears are soaking the bandages that cover the burns that run from my hand to my shoulder.

"I'm okay." But I know how I must look. I haven't showered yet, and soot is thick over the areas not bound or cast.

She releases my hand enough for the orderly to pass through into the hospital room where I'll stay for the next few days, and then my mom waits for him to leave.

In the next bed over, an old woman breathes through a chest tube. I wish I qualified for the pediatric ward where it would be kids and bright colors. The only flowers here whither in a yellow vase next to the old woman's bed. Silence and wheezes fill the room until my mom draws a deep breath.

"Why'd you do it?" she asks. "What happened? Why didn't you tell me about Fenwick?"

So I explain about Shadownet and where it came from. I tell her about Ellie and Tule and Harry and Hairy. I explain the missing abortion clinic laptop and about how the anonymous website really wasn't mine. I say how I couldn't tell her because she'd go to the police and the police would fine her, or worse, for not destroying the hard drives. I tell her about Jonny's ultimatum and how everything made sense at the time. But it all went wrong.

"And now you've sold the business to Fenwick," I cry. "What are we going to do?"

"I don't care about the business," she says. "I'll find something else."

"Mom, you don't have the money to start anything else and ..." I look at the wheelchair.

"Of all the people who should know better," she whispers. "You know I can still do whatever I want." Her eyes cloud—not a filmy, senile cloud, rather a-storm-is-here cloud.

"I know," I say.

"And if I didn't know how to overcome a challenge myself, then you've certainly showed me how this week."

"What do you mean?" I look up.

"Don't you realize how amazing you are?" Her expression makes me shift around on the bed. "The app development, this

Canvas—Peter says you've had thousands of downloads, it's going viral—and hacking into someone's WiFi, tracking down dangerous criminals. I can't condone it, but it's amazing."

"But I—" *I almost died*, I was about to say. "Thousands?"

"Thousands," she says. "And yes, what you did was dumb and you're grounded for a year. But it was also very brave and smart." She takes up my hand again. I'm so confused. "I was worried about you, who you were going to become, but Peter says I was worried about the wrong thing. I need to support you more. Support this passion of yours. If I had, maybe I'd have been able to help you do all this the right way."

She laughs and I'm stunned.

"This Shadownet of yours," she continues. "It wasn't really those other people. It's you, pieces of you fragmented on the Internet, but together it's you. And it's full of friendship and fans and followers. You're very lucky. I'm very lucky."

It's funny because I'm not so sure she's right. I do think of the Internet as real and the people on it are real, but it's like there is a level of reality I'm missing. One of flesh and blood.

I lean over, feeling my skin stretch and crack like I've had the worst sunburn ever. I wrap my arms around my mom's neck and kiss her cheek. "I love you," I say. And it's been a long time since I've told her so. "But I still want to nail those bastards."

My mom draws back, her mouth pinched.

"And how do you intend to go about that?"

"I think I have proof of a felony, a real felony that wouldn't be traceable to us. I just need some time on Shadownet."

"I've already signed over the business." She says this carefully.

"You don't have my computers?"

"That was part of the deal."

I glare at her, but she holds up the palm of her hand. "You were in a burning house and kidnapped, Janus. What was I supposed to do?"

"You've got a key?" I ask.

"Yes."

"I have to get back in, just for a minute."

"No way," she shakes her head. "You're hopped up on pain killers and are thinking crazy. Fenwick, whoever he is, has connections."

I slump back in my bed. The hard line of my mother's lips makes me realize I'm in over my head again. I need help.

"Do you trust me?"

My mother narrows her eyes, but nods.

"Can you find me a laptop?" I ask. "For homework," I add with a coy smile.

"Right," she says, "I guess I can manage that."

I push my luck. "And I need your phone."

She reaches to the back of her chair and pulls it out, but it's not her old clunker, it's an iPhone.

"Yeah, Mom!"

"It's yours—or Peter's, rather. He wants you to have it. Said you should see what people are creating on top of Canvas. Get some rest," she says. She rolls to the door and then pauses. "I love you too."

I settle on to my pillow and turn away from my wheezing bunkmate. After a few minutes I turn to a touch on the shoulder and open my eyes. It's like I've gone to Heaven. Karl's face shines beside a bouquet of roses.

"Hey," I say. "My hero."

He beams.

"How are you doing?" He places the flowers on the side table and sits on the edge of my mattress.

"Pretty good really," I say. "Ankle still hurts but they keep feeding me stuff if the pain gets too bad."

"Rough." His hand slips across the sheets to hold mine.

I realize I need to say or do something. I've always liked Karl, but— "Karl," I squeeze his hand and then let go. His smile twitches off kilter. "Can we be friends for a bit? I need friends right now."

He cracks his neck before responding and pats the spot where my hand had been. "Sure," he says. "We can be friends."

"Thanks." I swallow hard. "And for the flowers too, they're pretty."

"Something beautiful," he replies.

We sit for another minute in silence before he stands and leaves with only a wave.

It was hard, but I feel good about it.

Four hours later, I have a laptop. A scratched-up Dell, but to me it's a thing of beauty; it's a prosthetic limb. My mom has also left me my copy of *The Bell Jar*.

By the time Constable Williams enters the room, I've got everything I need.

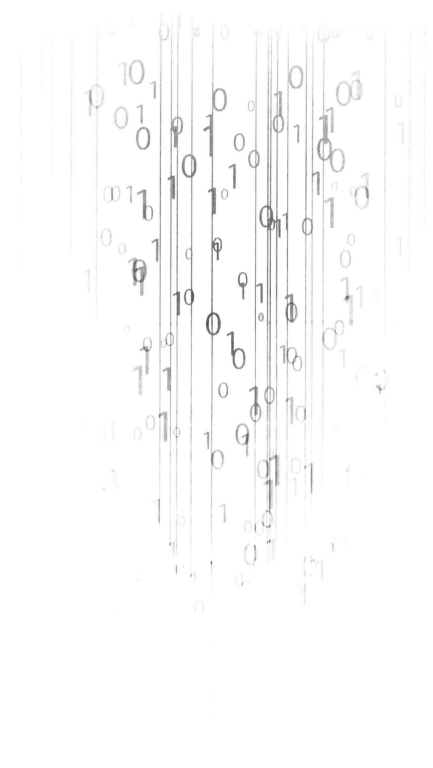

CHAPTER 24

01100100011000010111001001101011011100110110110001101001010110
11100110011101100101011100100010111001101110011001010101110100

"**W**HAT CAN I HELP YOU with, *Ms.* Rose?" Williams demands from the doorway. Her arms are folded across her chest.

Hmmm. I haven't made the best impression on this woman.

"I've evidence of child pornography," I say and nod toward the laptop.

She steps further into the room and peers at my computer screen. It simply reads: *Server not found.*

"Looks like the server is down."

"Yes," I say, "If I'm correct, the server that used to house this webpage is from a certain house that recently burned to the ground." I pause to see if she knows what I'm getting at, but she's unreadable. "But ... if I search Google and pull up the cached site from before the server burned ..." Google keeps an image of all the sites it crawls, so even if you can't connect to it directly, you can usually see what *was* there. "Now check this out."

She cracks her neck and her eyes sparkle with sudden interest. "That's the girl from your school, isn't it?"

The page is the same page I found when searching for the naked photo of Astrid. The same photo Harry allegedly posted.

"Astrid," I agree. "But this one isn't from Harry's Facebook page." And here's what I suspect. Fenwick couldn't resist adding Astrid's picture to his despicable collection. An underage picture.

"So who hosts the site?" Constable Williams asks. "Is this what was on the servers in the house fire you were in? Is this why you were there?"

"How much time would someone do for possessing child pornography?" I ask.

She shrugs. "Depends, but in this case we're looking at possession and dissemination of child pornography. That's more. Could be as much as twenty to thirty years in prison."

I nod. The fact that the porn site's server is down is too much of a coincidence for Fenwick not to have been involved, but it won't be enough for Constable Williams. She needs the smoking gun and I know where there's lots of smoking stuff. But that might be a problem.

"So?" she demands, taking out a pad of paper and pencil.

"If there's a fire, say ..." I lick my lips; my tongue rubbing painfully over the cracked edges. "Can you recover computer files from a server or computer?"

She sighs. "If the damage isn't too bad, but generally yes, we can recover a surprising amount, but it's expensive so we don't normally do it unless there's suspected foul play. You *are* talking about the house fire."

All my searches on the Web turned up the same thing. But Google is sometimes closer to Hollywood than to the realities of a true computer forensics team. So, not easy, but possible— there may be evidence of Fenwick's wrong doing yet. Best of all, it won't be tied to me or my mom.

"I believe you'll find photos of Astrid on the servers of the house that burned down," I say, and I sag into my pillows as if it's a huge weight taken from me.

"Wait a minute. You're the one who called the tip line?" Williams's hands are at her hips. "I knew there was something more to your involvement in all of this. You called about screaming in a car trunk?"

Damn her powers of deduction. I clear my throat. My voice rasps and I try to sound as pathetic as I can. "Just a coincidence," I say. It is an *anonymous* tip line. What I need to do is give her something she can prove.

Her face remains stony.

"In the basement of the house is a rack of servers and other old computer towers. Recover the files on them and you'll have all the proof you need to book two criminals."

Williams taps her pen back on her legal pad. "Okay, I'll check it out."

On her way through the door, she passes my mother, who wheels in without a word.

"You tell her what you told me?" my mom asks.

I shake my head vigorously and a shadow of disappointment darkens her expression.

"Do you have everything you need?" she asks.

"Hope so," I reply, running my hand through my stringy hair. My room is full of balloons and flowers and a humongous teddy bear from Karl, but nothing from Jonny. Even the wheezing woman is off of her chest tube and smiles between rather gooey meals and lets me watch whatever I want on television.

"Can I go see Peter?" I ask.

"I think he'd like that." My mom beams again, and right then, I can tell she's falling in love. For once I say the right thing.

"I'm happy for you, Mom. He's a great guy. I have a good

gut instinct for these things."

"Do you?" She laughs.

I feel my cheeks heat thinking of my own disastrous love life. One Everest at a time, I tell myself.

Peter has a bandage wrapped around his head and suffers from a severe concussion. He gets waves of headaches, but they're growing a little duller and less frequent. His hands press against his temples when I enter in my wheelchair. He calls us *the twins* and looks a little frail under all the blankets. It reminds me how much older he is, but then I remember him giving Fenwick an uppercut.

"You all right?" he asks.

"I still can't believe you follow me on Twitter," I say to change the subject.

He shakes his head slowly. "I don't."

"Then how'd you find out where I—"

"Jonny called your mom. He was worried when you didn't meet him."

"Jonny," I whisper and look around for him as if he should be here. Into my mind flashes an image of Karl's strong jaw, his blue eyes. I can still feel the power in his arms as he carried me.

"Your mom was furious that you'd lied again and asked for my help to find you. I hacked your account." Peter had the decency to wince in apology. "I looked through your last emails, saw the one about the app, and uploaded it to my iPhone. It did the rest."

"So you're a hacker?"

"I like to call it Internet security specialist, but yes, one of the best ways to test your security is to have a hackfest on it. I've hacked some of the biggest sites in the world."

"Ha! Can I maybe join a hackfest sometime? It sounds like fun."

"Lots of pizza," he says.

"Mom said you didn't do pizza."

"There's a lot your mom doesn't know about me," he says with a smile, which turns to a grimace as his face clenches in pain.

"Let's let Peter get some rest," my mom says and he doesn't try to dissuade us from leaving.

As I hustle along in my wheelchair, my mom keeps easy pace in hers. "You know, honey." She begins. "When the police officer comes back, you have a chance to come clean on everything else. Shadownet."

I stop wheeling and turn to her. "What about Fenwick's threat?"

"If the police can arrest Fenwick on the child pornography charges, we don't need to worry about that."

It's true—I can't think of a way he could trace the police finding child porn on his server to me. That was his dumb move.

"But if they found out I didn't destroy hard drives, you lose Assured Destruction."

"We all have to take responsibility for our actions, Janus." She kisses me goodbye at the elevator and I continue on to my room, but before I reach it I turn back.

"Mom, will you ever tell me what happened to you and Dad?" I ask.

She's counting the floors illuminated on the digital display. When the doors open, she smiles and says, "Is it okay to have some secrets, love?" She rolls into the elevator car and cranes her neck to look back over her shoulder. "You'll just have to trust me too." And the doors shut.

Back in my bed, it's getting late in the day, and dinner is peas, mashed potato, and Salisbury steak. I flick through TV channels to distract myself from the taste of the starchy goo, and later a nurse changes the dressings on my arms. I start rereading *The Bell Jar*, but the nurse must have given me something in the IV because I don't remember anything more until I wake up with Constable Williams nearly sitting in my lap. She's smiling.

"I've got an idea," she says.

I rub my eyes.

"You're pretty handy with computers, I take it."

"I ... uh ..."

"I interviewed your computer science teacher, says you're the smartest student he's ever had. You make him nervous."

I don't know why, but this makes me sad. Here I was, trying to figure out ways to torment the guy, and I make him nervous?

"Did you find—?"

"The pornography?" She nods her head up and down and looks far off in the distance. "Sure did. Including Astrid's picture. We've enough to convict him, Boris Kniezev, if we can find him."

"And you can't." So he'd used an alias. I figured this might happen, but my stomach does a little flip at the prospect of Assured Destruction being ours again. It's not much, but it's ours.

"I'm supposed to ask you questions about what you were doing in his house." She eyes me and I wait for the shoe to drop.

I remember what my mom said. About it being my choice and about taking responsibility. I figure there really is a right way and wrong way to do this. I shake my head.

"Can I tell you *everything* that happened? What I did?" I ask.

She grows serious and takes out her notepad again. I look at it and then begin. I tell her everything. Everything up to the kidnapping because I don't want Fenwick—Boris—to have some way of coming back at us—for wanting revenge. I've had my revenge. It was poetic enough for me.

When I'm done, Williams's smile expands further. "You're even better than I thought. To set the trap on the blog you would have had to write the trojan virus in an hour."

Twenty minutes, actually, but I keep my mouth shut.

"I won't say there won't be any repercussions for all of this, but I'm glad you told me. I wouldn't have decided to help you otherwise."

"It clears Harry and Astrid, right?" I struggle to sit up in the bed.

"Yes, and it might help us find the possessions of the Wise family."

"What punishment do you think I'll get?" I ask. "Will I do time?"

She chuckles. "Yes, you will, but how about we come up with a plan to present to the judge?"

"Sure," I say, not understanding, but glad for the help and scared to death of the word *judge*.

"I need to talk to my lieutenant, so you'll have to wait a bit." She pats my leg. "It won't be easy."

I still have no idea what she's talking about, but the image of court bangs around in my head, causing havoc.

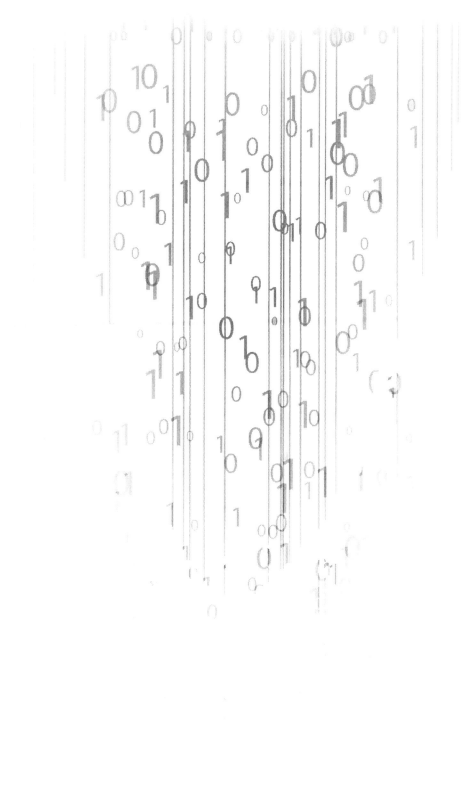

CHAPTER 25

0110010001100001011100100010110101101110011011011000110100101 10
1110011001110110010101110010000101110011011011001100101011101 00

W E ALL STAND AS THE judge enters. I'm trembling, glad for the crutches under my armpits that keep me from falling. My mom couldn't be here, but she asked Peter to pick me up. I'm all alone and in some ways I guess that makes sense to me. This is my crime. My justice.

Upright, my foot throbs. After four weeks, my dressings are off, but skin still sheds from my arms. The doctors don't think there will be scarring, but for now I'm scaly and molting.

The judge sits in his big pine pedestal box and everyone else settles into their seats. The two witness boxes on either side of him are empty, but a group of prisoners await trial on the far left hand side. Behind me half the seats are filled with people, most of whom I don't know with the exception of Constable Williams.

The first trial on the docket, I stand before the judge. The timing is a small gift since my nerves are already shot—except it looks as though this judge just woke up. He runs his hand across bag-saddled eyes and then puts on a pair of wire-rimmed reading glasses that make him look like an evil cartoon character.

Another woman in uniform—the clerk, I guess—hands him a case file and the judge rubs his hands together. I wonder if he's wearing underwear beneath his robes. I wouldn't. He glares down at me. It's already been a day of judgment. I had time to stop by school and meet with Principal Wolzowski before heading to court.

That meeting could have been worse. By confessing to everything, I'm cleared of the cyberbullying and neither Astrid's nor Harry's families will press charges. Ellie's, on the other hand, wants their paperback books and everything back and I can't help them. I didn't rob them! Half of it might have gone up in flames for all I know. This is what insurance is for, isn't it?

Wolzowski says I can't shake the plagiarism charge, but my suspension is over following my weeks of convalescence. At least I'm not expelled. The principal even made a little joke. He claimed that my new essay was plagiarized too, said it came from a conversation amongst people on Twitter, a blogger, and other social network updates. I couldn't believe it and objected, but he started laughing, admitting he followed Heckleena too.

I left the school a bit dumbstruck and actually looking forward to going back. I even caught sight of Karl, who waved and looked like he wanted to talk to me, but I kept going—not wanting to be late for court. I caught his text thirty seconds later: *Good luck today.*

I still haven't replied. I wonder for a moment if I've made the wrong decision. Unfortunately Jonny's already made up his mind. He called me a freak and hasn't spoken to me since. Which reminds me—he hadn't gone to the police, had he? Not even after I missed his deadline.

"Ms. Rose?" The judge is glowering at me.

"Yes, ma'am. Sir, I mean," I say. Someone chuckles.

"I asked you a question."

I have no idea what he asked. "Yes," I say.

"Yes, then go ahead."

"Yes, can you repeat the question, please?"

"Would you care to sit down?"

I gratefully fold on to the chair. I don't have a lawyer or anything. I've already pled guilty to the charges of mischief.

"Is Constable Williams here?" the judge asks, peering around.

She stands and he nods, urging her forward with a finger.

"You've agreed to sponsor the community service hours of Ms. Rose?"

"Yes, Your Honor." She glances back to me as she says so.

"Would you tell the court what this will entail?"

I lean forward because to be honest I don't even know. All the constable and I discussed was that I'd be helping her out. I assume filing and stuff. Maybe I'll need to shine everyone's shoes? Clean toilets?

"Janus Rose is a computer expert."

I blink.

"She will be working under me in the cyber security task force, rebuilding computers to create profiles of our suspects and designing software that will help us bring them down."

The judge sits back and takes off his glasses, peering at her as if to determine if she's sane. He then cocks his head a little.

"Well, who am I to stand in the way of fighting crime." He points a long finger at me. "You agree to this?"

It's tough to see through the tears filling my eyes, and a knot twists in my stomach so hard that I can't speak. I manage a vigorous nod.

"You've committed some serious missteps, Ms. Rose, broken privacy regulations, caused the distribution of intensely private information by retaining it when it should have been destroyed, or at the very least recycled."

And here it comes. The judgment.

"But this is all in the context of bringing down your very first criminal, I take it?"

The constable nods the affirmative. "Two, in fact. They are still at large."

"I don't want to see you headed in the wrong direction, Ms. Rose." The judge scratches out something on a legal pad. It looks like he's struggling with the math, finally he looks up. "I sentence you to two thousand hours of community service to be served after school hours and on weekends under the direction of Constable Williams or whosoever she determines to be appropriate." The gavel slams down. "Welcome, Ms. Rose, to the right side of the law." The clerk hands a new manila folder to the judge.

Everything is a blur. Williams helps me to my foot, and I crutch out of the court room in silence. Two thousand hours. I didn't expect the judge to be lenient, but two thousand hours? There was the small matter of obstruction of justice and my fake tip to the so-called anonymous tip line. But this seemed a bit stiff. If I manage two hours a day and five on each weekend day, it'll take me … I do the math … two years! I'll finish up somewhere around my high school graduation.

"Welcome to the force," Williams says.

I have never been a slave before. How am I supposed to help my mom with the business, especially now that Fenwick is gone? I start to grow angry, but then I remember what the constable said to the judge. I'd be profiling suspects, bringing them down.

I design apps. I create people out of their hard drives, but I never really knew why. I had no real purpose. And now I do. I'm like a geeky superhero.

"Do I get a gun?"

"Only digital ones. Do you realize the computing power we have access to?" There's a sly smile on her face.

"Let's go fight crime," I say.

I laugh, and we push through the doors to the court house, where I freeze.

"Can I give you a ride home in my cruiser?" Constable Williams asks.

I'm staring at Jonny. He's skipping class again.

"Or ... would you like to make your own way home," she adds. I know she sees what I see. Jonny's got something in his hand, something wrapped up.

"Own way, please," I manage.

I crutch toward him, he's staring at me.

"Hey," I say—brilliant conversationalist that I am, but this guy's last word to me was *freak*.

"What'd the judge give you?" He holds out the gift. It's a small cylinder and I guess what it is without opening it.

"Is that yellow?" I ask. I don't have anywhere to put it, but grab hold of the present anyways.

He blushes.

"Thanks—sweet," I say. "I got two thousand hours of community service with the police."

"Whoa, bummer, eh?"

"No, I deserve it," I say. "I'm going to be their White Hat Hacker." It's not a job title Williams gave me, but I like it.

"Drive you home?" he asks.

I look around. "Peter's supposed to pick me up."

"Your mom called and asked me to."

"Wha—I mean, cool." I can't believe my mom set this up. I'm going to kill her.

We don't talk as I crutch to his car; it's tough going and the foot still hurts. But he must have been stewing the whole time we walked, wanting to say something, because when we reach his car he suddenly bursts out with: "Are you and Karl?"

I've got both my crutches in one hand and I lose my balance and tumble, waving my arms toward the car.

Pain lances through my foot. "Am I and Karl *what*?" I ask from the ground.

"You know—together." He bends down to grab my hand. It's the first time he's touched me since a rainy night weeks ago. I've had time to get over Jonny. Karl even sent a teddy bear with the flowers instead of spray paint—although spray paint is definitely cooler.

"We're not together," I say.

And he pulls me up, staying close. I see the stubble around his jaw and above his lip. It's cute, and his lip protrudes in a way that makes me want to kiss it. He backs up a step and I wobble again, but at least I manage to lean on the car while he opens the back door to help me inside.

The whole scenario is a bit pathetic, because it's easier for me to lie down in the back than it is to climb into the front seat. So we pass the drive with me feeling like my mother is driving me home rather than my ... what?

We're close to home when I remember a question: "How did Fenwick get your computer?"

He looks at me in the rearview mirror and his eyes are just like Paradise57's.

"When I came around to see you a few months ago. A big guy chased me away, but I dropped my backpack. I wasn't totally sure what was in it, and I was so embarrassed I couldn't ask you at school. The guy had said he'd drop me in the shredder if he caught me."

I cringed, hearing my orders repeated from Jonny.

"It was really old anyways," he continued. "I just told my mom it had stopped working."

"If I'd only come clean sooner …" I said, half to myself.

He parks well away from the front entry, on the opposite side of Assured Destruction's lot. I wonder why; doing so forces me to crutch an extra hundred yards I'd rather not have to cross.

"I want to show you something," he says.

He pulls out his iPhone and I catch the icon for Canvas, which looks like a Jackson Pollock painting. When it's loaded he hands the phone over to me.

"What you did for me," he says and wrenches his lips back and forth as if sampling the words. His Adam's apple bobs as he swallows. "What I'm trying to say is, people don't do nice things for me. This—" He chokes on the word and motions to the phone.

I tap the viewer and bring it up, scanning for graffiti. I don't need to look far.

"—it's the nicest thing anyone has ever done for me," he says. "You've made the whole world my canvas."

I'm looking out the back window of his car, unable to speak. Great stems grow up from the pavement and burst over the wall in a firework of petals and colors. Amongst the foliage, elves and gnomes play. He's turned our drab block of a warehouse into a wild, fantastic jungle. My mom's there in her wheelchair, and I am too, swinging on a vine with flowers in my hair and eyes shining. My home is a paradise. I guess it always has been.

"We're even," I say. "This is the nicest thing anyone has ever done for me."

I turn back to him and his eyes hold me. I nearly fall off the back seat but manage to shift forward enough to give him an indication of what I want. I lean forward and touch my lips to his. It's a dry brush, but it's wonderful. It's a real kiss, our first shared kiss and there's only ever one. I smile and do something I've always wanted to do. I run my fingers into his hair.

We kiss deeply until I pull back. My gut tells me this is right. Or maybe it's not my gut, maybe it's my heart.

"Your mural's missing something, though," I say. I turn to the app and zoom in on a bare area of the mural. Then I choose my color—yellow. And proceed to draw a yellow stickman, with shaggy brown hair and a spray can in one hand.

I choose Jonny; after all, I am now a representative of the police, and I think they'd prefer I go for the boy who likes me for me, rather than for being a bad girl—an image I might have trouble keeping up. We make out a little longer until I see my mom knocking on the storefront window so hard I'm afraid she'll break it.

I leave Jonny in the car and hobble over to my mom, who opens the door.

"Peter's taking us out for a celebratory lunch," she says. "Go get changed."

"Sure, Mom, sounds great." And it does. The realization that I'd gained a lot out of this strikes me hard. I have my mom back and I even like her nearly worm-food boyfriend. I draw her close to me and deliver a great hug. "I just have one thing I want to do."

The stairs down to Shadownet are the same as they always have been, but they seem foreign to me now. It's darker down here. The air that slips up past my thighs seems cooler as I use the rail to hop from step to step on my good leg. No hum soothes the concern from my brow. I crutch to Gumps's console. He's still here, blinking green as ever. Dependable.

Beside it is my backpack, and I see Peter's hard drive sticking out. I pull the hard drive and flip it a few times in the air. I'd forgotten about it. I should really spagettify the thing. Peter saved my life. But then I also remember him slamming Fenwick into the wall and delivering an uppercut. It had looked … practiced. I bite my lip and shove his hard drive deep inside the pack. Later. I'll shred it later. Instead I turn to Gumps and type.

8-ball question: Should I recreate Shadownet?

Answer: She who overcomes others is strong; she who overcomes herself is mighty.

I have a suspicion that whatever question I asked, I would have got the same answer. I turn to Paradise57's terminal. It's dark too, and I leave it that way, opening up the tower housing and unscrewing the hard drive. I nod to myself as I climb the stairs back to the store and punch the big green button that sits like a beauty mark beside Chop-chop's lips. The shredder roars to life and I toss the hard drive into its mouth, turning Paradise57 into strings of metal. My ankle is throbbing with all the activity. As I turn off Chop-chop, a baby blue Mercedes pulls to the front of the store.

"Lock the door as you leave," my mom says with a proud grin.

It's Saturday afternoon and Assured Destruction is closed for a family day.

I take a final look at the dark interior before crutching into the light. Almost immediately my phone rings and I give Mom and Peter an apologetic smile.

"Go on," my mom says.

It's the Ottawa Police Department.

"Hello, constable," I say and my voice squeaks.

"We need you, Janus. As soon as you can get here. There's been a terrible crime."

01000101011011100100

I hope you enjoyed Book 1 of the Assured Destruction Series. If you did, please be sure to let others know on Amazon, Barnes and Noble, or wherever you purchase or review books. To learn more about the series or to connect with other readers and the author, join us on Facebook!

01100001011101010111010001101000011011110110010

After crewing ships in the Antarctic and the Baltic Sea and some fun in venture capital, Michael anchored himself (happily) to a marriage and a boatload of kids. Now he injects his adventurous spirit into his writing with brief respites for research into the jungles of Sumatra and Guatemala, the ruins of Egypt and Tik'al, paddling the Zambezi and diving whatever cave or ocean reef will have him. He is a member of the International Thriller Writers and SF Canada, and the author of the Assured Destruction series, 24 Bones, The Sand Dragon, Hurakan, Ruination and several award winning graphic novels for young adults. Find out more about him on his website.

**01000001011000110110101101101110011011110111
01110110110001100101011001000011001110110010
10110110101100101011011100111010001110011**

Where to start? This project is huge, spilling far beyond the edges of these pages. With the blogging, the art, the cover, the tweets and Facebooking, the editing, and all of the incredible support, I'm bound to miss someone.

So I'll bend a knee in no particular order. To my wife and family for the freedom to do what I do. Thank you. To Kendra Brown, Alexandra Williams and the Writer's Workshop for your beta reads. To Catherine Adams of Inkslinger Editing, please, keep on slinging. You're amazing. To Michele Mortimer for your editing, agenting and for believing in this project. To Don Dimanlig for your art, artistry and inspiring graphics. To Janak Alford of PrototypeD for everything technical and for making the Assured Destruction storyworld come to life. And to Julie Giles of Green Hat Digital for getting the word out. Thank you all.

And back to my wife, Andrea. I dedicate this book to you.

CPSIA information can be obtained at www.ICGtesting.com
Printed in the USA
LVOW05s1615311013

359480LV00003B/633/P